FORCED TO BE QUEEN

LOLA GLASS

To average humans

AVALON ISLAND

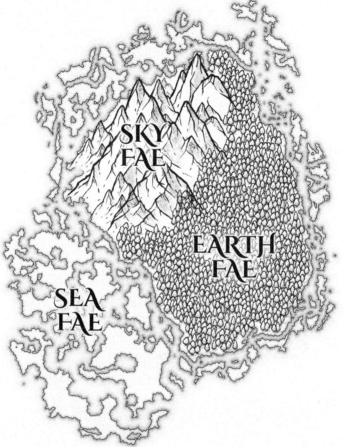

Chapter 1

"Three of the fae will escort you home to grab your things," the government employee said, somehow maintaining a neutral expression as I stared at him with my mouth hanging open like I was a fish waiting to be hooked in the cheek.

"How—" I choked on the words. "How was this decided?"

"Names were drawn at random." The man was skinny, middle-aged, and balding... and completely unsympathetic.

"I was never notified, or—"

"No one was notified. It would've created mass hysteria."

"Okay, but—"

The doors swung open, and I spun around. Three massive men strode into the room, each of them with hair and eyes the colors of gemstones.

Fae.

They looked insanely out of place in the bland government office with its tan walls and décor that would've been in-style fifteen years ago.

My mouth opened and closed a few times; my resemblance to a fish was growing. You know, minus the faded t-shirt, cutoff shorts, and pale skin.

"This has to be illegal." I spun back toward the balding guy. His eyes were on the fae, and now, he was sweating. "I was told I had to come in for an interview for the wife thing. No one said I was already chosen."

"This is the girl?" one of the fae asked, his voice heavy with disdain.

I glanced at them again.

The fae at the front of the group had green hair and dark skin. The two flanking him were tan, one with yellow hair, and the other with blue. The green-haired one at the front was the one who'd done the talking.

"Yes. She won't be missed." The balding man nodded.

My jaw fell open again.

I didn't give a crap if I resembled a fish; I'd just been told that the country had sold me to the fae. Granted, it was for a good cause, but that didn't mean I was okay with it.

"You'll be seen as a hero," the government-guy told me, not even a hint of apology in his voice. "Your sacrifice will save the world."

"*My* sacrifice? I never volunteered to be here."

A tree-trunk-sized arm wrapped around my middle, and I went airborne before my face crashed into a disgustingly-muscular back. Luckily, it was covered in a white t-shirt, even if said t-shirt was thin and ultra-tight.

I started to yell for help, but a deep-yellow eye appeared in my line of sight, blocking my view of the fae's ass and the floor. My voice cut off abruptly at the shock of the man's sudden appearance.

"She doesn't look strong," the yellow-eyed, yellow-haired fae announced. "She won't survive ten minutes in the presence of an angry king."

"She's as strong as any of our women," the balding man said. "As per our agreement, we gave you the most average human we could find."

Seriously? That was what qualified me for being sacrificed?

"She's average weight, and average height. Average pants and shoe size, too. Her hair is an average length as well as an average brown color, as are her eyes. There's no family to miss her. She made average grades in school, and has only completed a few college courses, as is also average."

"Why would a king want an average female?" The yellow-eyed fae's face twisted in disgust as he straightened, leaving me to look at the ugly tile floor and the chiseled backside of the fae holding me. "Our kings demand excellence."

The government employee looked like he was shaking a bit, but he wasn't backing down. "She fits the bills of our agreement. Do you wish to back out on the terms we agreed to?" There was a hint of a threat in his voice.

The third fae, the blue-haired one, grumbled, "The kings don't care about the quality of the women. Let's go."

Bastards.

All of them were bastards.

I peeled my face off the one fae's back as he turned, my accusing eyes turning on the balding jerk standing behind his desk. "This isn't right."

"What's necessary isn't always right," he said simply.

The door shut behind us as I struggled to straighten up more. Maybe I could gain some traction, and make a run for it, or—

The green-haired fae jerked me a bit, and my face slammed into his back again. The man-looking monster's body was like a boulder against my face.

Yeah, no. There was no way I could run away from them.

"You people seriously think I'm going to marry your king?" I asked, my voice wobbling.

"Unfortunately for him." The yellow-haired one smirked.

Real charming, the lot of them.

We passed empty hallways, empty desks, empty offices. Most businesses had shut down when the fae appeared a few weeks ago, and as far as I'd seen, none had fully started back up.

The fae carried me out into a parking garage, and then tossed me into the back seat of a sleek black SUV. I was positive it was part of the massive government payout the fae had been given.

Just like I was, apparently.

Before the fae portaled onto our planet, there had been world and government policies in place to prevent shit like this from happening. But then the fae had shown up. And now, the whole damn planet was scrambling.

We'd all seen the videos—the fae had portaled into the middle of San Francisco in a big, red, glowing cloud of what could only be magic. And then the tsunamis hit. And the earthquakes. And the storms.

The fae had somehow managed to make our planet destroy *itself* with unnatural natural disasters.

When they'd overtaken some little island in the Atlantic and claimed it as their own a few days after portaling in, the world's governments had offered them everything they could think of to convince them to end the days-long disasters. Money, power, expensive shit... the fae hadn't wanted anything.

What they did want?

Wives.

Three human women, to be exact.

The US had been hit by the disasters the hardest, so after two weeks of hellish storms, flooding, and all sorts of other shit, our government had agreed in a heartbeat.

The agreement had been finalized a week ago, and the storms ended, but life didn't resume as normal. All women between 21 and 30—the "peak reproductive age"—had our information taken from our doctors' offices, schools, and jobs. From there, we'd been told our names would be dropped in a lottery-style pool.

Similar to the draft, they'd said.

Apparently, that was bullshit.

"Address?" the blue-haired fae grunted. Green-Hair was in the driver's seat, with Blue-Hair in the passenger seat and

Yellow-Hair in the chair beside mine, and the car was still parked firmly in the garage.

It took me a minute to realize Blue-Hair was talking to me.

I rattled off my address, and the yellow-haired one stabbed at the screen of a phone as if it was trying to kill him or something.

New to technology, I guess.

Yellow-Hair cursed under his breath in a language I didn't recognize. Blue-Hair reached over the seat and plucked the device from the other fae's fingers.

"What was it?" He looked at me.

I repeated my address again, and Blue-Hair struggled to type it in. When he asked me to repeat it *again*, I spelled it out, letter by letter and number by number.

The fae hit the button to start the navigation, and the robotic female voice said, "You will arrive in one day and seven hours."

I snorted; I couldn't help it. My apartment was less than half an hour away. The fae just really sucked at technology, apparently.

Three sets of glaring eyes landed on me.

All of my humor vanished.

"Type it yourself," Blue-Hair growled, shoving the phone at me.

I took it from his hands, eyeing the fae while my fingers moved quickly over the screen. After a glance to make sure I'd typed correctly, I hit the button to start navigation.

"You will arrive in twenty-six minutes," the voice stated.

Relieved breaths relaxed all three of the oversized-men, and Yellow-Hair ripped the phone out of my hand. He stuck it on a mount, so Green-Hair could see it, and the fae finally turned the car on.

My eyes trailed glumly over my old Camry, sitting alone up against one of the other walls in the garage, as we pulled out of the parking lot. The car accelerated too quickly, and my body tensed as I grabbed the *oh-shit* handle above my head.

The next twenty-six minutes were some of the most terrifying in my life. Not because the fae drove fast—because they were shitty at it. Jerky turns, brakes slamming, moving in and out of the lane by accident... they were a mess.

Luckily, there were hardly any other cars on the road. Most people who were still alive were still trying to figure out what to do next. Picking up the pieces of our broken planet was easier said than done.

When the fae finally slammed on the brakes in front of my apartment building, the men looked up at the three-story building I called home.

"Well, at least she's wealthy," one of them muttered.

I couldn't help it; I snorted again.

They all looked at me.

"I'm not rich. It's an apartment building, not a mansion." Opening my door, I slid out of the car and headed up toward the staircase.

The fae shuffled up the small concrete staircase behind me.

"This is inhumane," one of the fae grunted.

The staircase was inhumane?

Coming from the fae who had wiped out hundreds of millions of people?

Yeah, right.

I unlocked my door, and they followed me inside. They remained by the door, speechless, as they looked over my little one-bedroom apartment.

It was clean, and there were a few decorations on the bland-looking walls and countertops—random stuff, some I'd brought from my grandpa's place after he passed and some that I'd collected. Nothing was matchy-matchy, or fancy, or coordinated in the slightest. The only nice thing in the apartment was the piano taking up most of the far-right corner in the living room; that gorgeous, dark-wood, upright instrument was my favorite thing that I owned.

And now that the world had ended and I'd been sacrificed to the fae, she was the only thing I'd miss.

"They've given us one of their prisoners," Green-Hair muttered.

I rolled my eyes as I stepped into my bedroom. Hopefully, I'd be back home soon, and life would resume as normal.

But that wasn't likely.

I grabbed my suitcase out from under my bed. It was an ancient thing, made of old black fabric, and inherited from my grandpa when he passed. We'd only ever gone on one vacation, so we'd never needed to spend the money on a better suitcase.

Unzipping it, I ignored the fae who moved to stand in the doorway. He stared at me while I put stuff in my bag.

I wasn't really attached to any of my clothing, and the government had made the fae rich, so I grabbed the things that did matter: the stuff I'd gotten from my grandpa.

Odds and ends filled the bag as I went in and out of my room, gathering them. A few tools and pocket knives, a couple of little trinkets, a handful of photo albums, and some wooden signs with sarcastic sayings on them that my grandpa had kept after my grandma died.

I threw in a phone charger and my laptop before grabbing a few pieces of clothing to top it all off just so I wouldn't be walking around naked if they refused to buy me clothes.

My heart started to beat faster when I glanced at the fae in the doorway.

I needed him to walk away for a minute.

"Can you grab me some water?" I asked. "It's in the fridge."

The fae scowled, but walked away.

Shoving my hand between my mattress and bed frame, my fingers wrapped around the cold metal of the handgun my grandpa had always insisted I keep.

Being sacrificed to the fae wasn't the only shitty thing that could happen to a woman, after all.

I tucked the gun and a few bullets into my bag, wrapping it in a sweatshirt so I knew it wouldn't make noise or anything.

The fae were insanely powerful, and had the magic to protect themselves from bombs and other kinds of flying weapons, but they were made of flesh and blood just like us humans. If this so-called *angry fae king* I was officially arranged to marry tried to do anything I wasn't on board with, I'd shoot him.

But that was definitely a last-resort plan. Shooting one fae would still leave me surrounded by a bunch of others.

Walking back out to the living room, I dropped my suitcase to the floor and yanked on the handle until it came up high enough for me to grab it.

One of the fae took it from me, smashing the handle back down with a gigantic, meaty fist and lifting the bag like it was a damned pillow. My lips formed an "O" as he propped it up on his shoulder like it weighed nothing.

With one last sad glance at my piano, I followed him out.

Chapter 2

After another terrifying drive, we made it to the airport. I was worried security would find my gun and tell the fae, but we were escorted past the security checkpoints and directly into a small private plane.

Despite being twenty-two, I'd never been on an airplane before. My fingers fiddled with the ring on a short chain around my neck as the plane took off. I didn't want to look at the flooded, broken world below our plane, but something about the sad state of everything drew my attention and wouldn't let go.

The fae left me alone, and I left them alone. It wasn't easy to pretend they weren't there, and that I wasn't leaving my ruined life at the crumbling governments' whim, but I tried.

When the plane landed and we were escorted off, I could no longer deny that I was in deep trouble—and that my entire life was about to change.

. . .

THE FAE LED me out of a crumbling airport. The building had caved in, and my throat swelled when I looked all of that destruction in the face. My little city in Nebraska had been hit by a two-week-long storm, but we'd narrowly dodged multiple tornadoes and had only dealt with small earthquakes. We'd been lucky; many others had not.

Particularly those by the ocean.

Trying to focus on the here-and-now instead of the awful fate of so many innocent people, I followed the broken sidewalk until it turned into a sandy path. The destroyed city we'd flown to was on the east coast somewhere, which meant it had been wiped out by one of the many tsunamis that had followed the fae's portal in.

My throat swelled further when I saw more destruction.

Broken trees, broken vehicles, broken homes...

So much wreckage.

At least if I was losing my life to the fae, it was for a good cause. To stop the disasters and the dying, I would've gone willingly. The government bastard was right; I had no family, no one who would miss me. If someone had to go with the fae, it may as well be me. But it was too bad the guy hadn't bothered just to *ask*.

I followed them to a dock that stretched a ways over a river, and out to the single big boat attached to the dock. I knew nothing about boats, but could tell it was a nice one.

I climbed into the boat, settling on a bench when the fae

pointed me over to it. Instead of starting the boat, the fae sat down on the bench across from mine and stared at me.

Three sets of creepy eyes stuck to my body, and I grimaced. I knew what they were seeing; five and a half feet of *average human woman*.

My light brown hair fell an inch past my collarbone, stick-straight and soft, although not thick by any definition of the word. My eyes were a simple brown color that my high school boyfriend had called "steady" as if that was supposed to make me feel gorgeous. I wasn't skinny, fat, or curvy; I fell somewhere in-between all that.

My cutoff shorts had started as full-length pants, and I'd taken scissors to them a few years earlier when the holes in the knees grew so massive I couldn't justify wearing them anymore. My shirt was a faded old tee from my grandpa's auto-repair shop, just like the others I'd shoved in my bag, and I couldn't remember if I'd swiped on mascara that morning or not.

The way I looked wasn't my priority. I didn't owe it to anyone to look pretty or sexy. I'd spent years focused on making enough money to stay alive until I could make money doing what I loved—playing the piano. If the fae assholes thought I was less because of that, they could swallow a damned wrench.

I ignored the staring fae for a while, but by the time ten minutes had passed, I was annoyed.

"What are we waiting for?" I asked the men.

"The other women," Green-Hair grunted.

The other women?

I knew the fae had made a deal for three human women with the government, but it was surreal to be one of them, waiting for the other two.

We descended back into silence and awkward stares, and waited.

A few minutes later, a pale, stressed girl who looked about my age came walking up behind three more monstrous fae. Like mine, her hair was a medium-brown color, though hers was a shade or two lighter.

Much like me, she wasn't fat or skinny, her boobs were an average size, and nothing about her screamed, "LOOK AT ME."

She slid onto the bench beside me, scooting so close that our bodies nearly touched. "What's your name?" she whispered.

"Noa Murphy. You?" I murmured back. My full name was November, but no one called me that. It was a mouthful, and I didn't particularly like being named after a calendar-month.

"Hannah Cooke." She gave me a hesitant smile, and it lit up her blue-gray eyes. "What are we doing?" Her gaze flicked back to the fae and her skin grew ashen, all light fading instantly.

Yeah, I felt that too.

"Waiting. I think there's only one more girl coming." I glanced at the fae, hoping for confirmation.

They didn't say anything, though they definitely kept staring.

I looked at Hannah. "Did you get any kind of a warning?"

Her expression grew frustrated. "No. They lied about why they asked me into the office, and didn't even let me pack a bag." Her face grew a bit red as her anger kicked up a notch. "I had to call a friend to go pick up my dog, and I don't know when I'll be able to go back for him."

I was pretty sure it was an "if" we'd be able to go back home, not a "when," but didn't want to upset her by saying so.

"Where are you from?" Hannah asked me.

"Nebraska. You?"

"Colorado."

There weren't many states that had been excluded from the monstrous tidal waves the fae had brought, but ours were among them.

"Did you call your family?" I checked.

"I don't have any family," she admitted.

"I don't either."

That wasn't a coincidence, though. The neutral government jerk had pointed my lack of family out alongside my *average* qualities.

"Do you think—" she began, halting when another set of colorful-haired fae came walking down the dock. There was another girl behind them; still average height and body-size, her hair a slightly-darker brown than mine or Hannah's.

Her expression was serious, but uncertain, as she slid onto the bench beside Hannah.

The fae got up and started the boat, pulling it away from

the dock as Hannah asked the newcomer the same things she'd asked me. We learned her name, Elyn Luther, and that she was from Wyoming.

The three of us *average women* were quiet through the long boat ride. I kept waiting for the fae to use their magic to make us move faster or something, but they didn't.

THE SUN WAS SETTING when the fae island was finally within view.

My lips parted as it grew closer. Small islands littered the ocean in front of the massive one, some sandy, some grassy, some with trees, and some completely bare. On the main island, Mountains stretched so high into the clear blue sky that I couldn't see the tops of them. In front of the lightly-forested mountains, there was a thick area of pine trees covering rolling hills.

"Wow," Hannah breathed beside me.

"I hate it more for being beautiful," Elyn muttered.

We passed a dozen more small islands before we made it to a dock set on the edge of the main, largest island. The dock was nestled right between the mountains and the thick forest, and while I didn't know why it had been done that way, the location seemed intentional.

"Follow us," Green-Hair barked, heading off the ship with a handful of others at his side. I'd spent enough time with that one already to know I didn't want to piss him off.

The three of us ladies exchanged grimaces, but followed.

We carefully made our way down the slanted metal

bridge-thing leading to the docks, and an orange-haired fae gestured for us to keep following before striding into the trees.

"My average-sized legs can't keep up with his," Hannah mumbled, as we jogged in an attempt to stay close to him.

I snorted. "Even an above-average human couldn't keep up with him."

Elyn made a noise of agreement.

Luckily we only had to jog for a few minutes before stopping, because I'd never liked the gym or any other form of physical exercise.

The group of fae we'd been following stepped up under a simple but massive wooden gazebo. In the center of it stood four other fae men that we hadn't met before.

It occurred to me then that I'd never seen any fae women, or kids—not on TV, or the internet, or even in person.

Where were they all?

We slowed to a walk as we reached the gazebo.

"Do you think those are the ones we're supposed to marry?" Hannah whispered.

I didn't know, but the idea made me sick. Marriage hadn't been on my radar—at all—and there I was, about to be trapped in a sham of a marriage with a fae king at twenty-two years old.

"I hope not," Elyn muttered back.

We approached the group of fae men. Now there were nine of them, with the addition of the ones we'd been following.

"Welcome, human women." One of the men spread his

arms out in front of him in a surprisingly-human gesture. He wasn't any older than any of the others around him; they all looked stuck in their mid-twenties.

None of us said anything.

What were we supposed to say? Thanks for having us? It wasn't like any of us had volunteered to be there.

My eyes quickly moved over the new group of men. All fae were giants—the shortest ones were six feet tall, according to the internet. These new ones had to be six-and-a-half feet or taller.

Green-Hair stood beside the one that greeted us. The greeter had thick, curly sapphire-blue hair and onyx-black eyes. Beside him stood two light-skinned men with the exact same shade of vibrant, ruby-red hair. The two of them looked similar, though one was a bit bigger and rougher-looking.

Beside the redheads stood an angry-looking pale-skinned fae with platinum-blonde hair, and oddly enough, eyes almost the exact same shade as his hair. I wasn't sure what gemstone he was supposed to resemble; a diamond, maybe?

The rougher-looking redhead stepped up to us and draped an arm over Hannah's shoulder. She made a small squeaking noise, and his lips curved up in a grin. "I'll take this one."

Elyn took a hasty step back.

I looked at the group of men, trying to figure out which of the others were the kings. There were supposed to be three of them, right?

"This is absolute bullshit," the blond fae growled. A wave

crashed against the dock, and all of us women jerked our heads toward it.

We turned just in time to watch the boat we'd ridden in get swept up in a wave. The wave drew it back... and then smashed it into the mountain beside the dock.

Yikes.

That guy had a temper, and could apparently control the water? He was probably one of the bastards responsible for the tsunamis, then.

"I'll take this one," the softer-looking redhead said, stepping beside Elyn without touching her.

Crap.

Unless one of the fae who'd come to retrieve us was a king—which seemed unlikely—the only other two possibilities were the blond fae, and the blue-haired one.

So I was praying I'd get to marry a dude with blue hair. Cool.

"Step up beside your bride," Blue-Hair said brightly, gesturing toward me.

Dammit.

Last pick, and stuck with the asshole with anger-issues. Why did this suddenly feel like high-school all over again?

The blond guy stalked over to me, and I ignored the instinct telling me to step away from him. If my *husband* thought he could scare me into doing things, life would be much more difficult for me.

The third king stepped between me and Elyn. Other than his insane size and weird whitish-silverish eyes, he looked just like a human. None of the fae even had pointy ears; it was weird.

"What are your names?" the blue-haired fae prodded.

When we didn't answer, the green-haired one I'd traveled with reached into his pocket, pulling out a couple of folded sheets of paper. He handed the papers to the blue-haired fae.

Blue-Hair's eyes scanned the paper. "Elyn Luther?"

Elyn raised her hand a tiny bit, and the blue-haired one gave her an encouraging smile before looking at the softer of the two redheads, who stood beside her. "Sign the empty line, Merzo."

The fae took the paper and a pen from the blue-haired guy, used his knee as a table, and signed the thing before handing it back.

I guess even fae had to be creative sometimes.

"Don't I need to sign?" Elyn asked, her voice less worried now.

I wasn't surprised that she was calmer; she seemed to have gotten the better-end of the fae-husband deal. Quiet, and respectful of personal space. Could an arranged marriage get any better?

"You signed when you filled out paperwork for your government," the blue-haired fae said cheerfully.

My lips parted.

They'd had us sign a marriage license? How the hell had I missed that? The stack of papers had been monstrous, but I'd tried to read everything.

Elyn and Hannah looked just as shocked by the revelation as I was.

"Hannah Cooke?" the blue-haired one looked between me and Hannah.

Following Elyn's example, Hannah raised her hand.

"Perfect. Kalus, this is yours." He gave the paper to the redhead with an arm around Hannah, and the redhead somehow managed to scribble his name on the page without removing his arm from her shoulders.

"And that makes you November Murphy." Blue-Hair smiled at me.

I definitely didn't return the smile.

"What kind of name is November?" the fae beside me grunted. "Isn't that a month?"

The words annoyed me, so I spoke when I shouldn't have. "What kind of man marries a woman who doesn't want him?" I shot back.

The gazebo went silent for a moment.

The blond king crumpled the paper in his hand and dropped it and the pen to the ground. It was too late though; he'd already signed it.

He spun to face me, silver eyes furious and chest rising and falling rapidly.

Yeah, I shouldn't have gotten pissy.

The ocean crashed violently against the mountains, destroying the dock and washing it away as the blond king strode toward the expanse of water.

"Wist, Chaos," Kalus, the rougher fae, growled, and looked at the blue-haired fae. "I'll talk to him. Get them ready for the first power transfer, Ien." He headed off in the direction Chaos, the angry blond, had gone.

I didn't know what a power transfer was.

Did I want to find out?

Not really. It didn't sound *good*.

But I doubted I'd get a choice in the matter, being an *average human*.

"Follow me," the blue-haired fae's smile looked far more forced as he gestured toward the trees.

I guess he was Ien.

The third king slipped away as Ien grabbed the paper Chaos had dropped, leaving us alone with the blue-haired and green-haired fae men.

Green-Hair took up the back of the group, while Ien led us down a dirt path that cut through the forest.

"Way to piss off the scary one," Elyn muttered to me as we walked.

"It's a talent," I agreed.

Though I felt bad that the other human women were on the receiving end of some anger because of my actions, they weren't the ones paired up with a guy called *Chaos*. If he was going to hate anyone, it would be me. And if he thought I was someone he could abuse, he was going to find out the hard way that I was the kind of girl who hit back.

Hard.

CHAPTER 3

WE'D BEEN WALKING for twenty or thirty minutes when we finally turned down a smaller dirt path. The trees grew sparser as we walked, until we found a massive building nestled into the trees.

The building looked like it was carved out of stone, towering a few stories above our heads and spreading out widely to my left and right. The top of it looked to be tucked between the trees, just barely tall enough not to show through.

"This is King Kalus's castle," Ien explained as he led us up to the giant doors.

I tried to remember which of the redheads was Kalus, but drew up a blank.

"He's Hannah's husband, and King of the Earth Fae. They control rock and stone, along with soil and precious metals," Ien added.

Ah. The rougher of the two redheads.

"Will we be expected to live with our husbands?" Elyn asked. "And share beds with them?"

It was a good question... but I wasn't sure I wanted to know the answer.

Mainly because there was a chance I'd really, really hate it.

"You'll share their homes, but not their beds. Our kings have married you out of duty, the same reason you married them."

I scowled. There had been no duty involved for us—only trickery.

But at least the kings didn't want us for our bodies; that was far better than the alternative.

"What's the power transfer that Kalus mentioned?" Hannah asked.

"Fae—the males of our people—cannot open portals into Avalon. Only out of it. We need faeries to open a portal back into our homeland," he explained as he opened the door to the mansion, holding it open for us.

Shock hit me hard, and I stopped on the porch, just outside the door.

They needed faeries.

Meaning... "You want to turn us into fae?"

"Not completely. Only to enough of a degree that the land will open a portal for you." He smiled, like that made it okay. "To do that, someone needs to give you part of their magic. In my visions, I saw that it would only work if it was the kings."

My lips parted. "Visions, as in..."

"Yes, I see bits and pieces of the future," he confirmed.

Wow.

Crap.

I didn't want to become like them, not even a little. They'd killed so many people, screwed our world over so badly that I didn't know if we could even recover.

But what could I do to stop it?

If they needed faeries to get them back home, they wouldn't stop until they had them.

Them, meaning *us*.

"Right this way," the fae said, gesturing us down a hallway.

I finally stepped into the building. Despite the warm, tropical weather outside, the building was cold and musty. It smelled like wet dirt, and my nose wrinkled at the unpleasantness of it.

"At least it smells good in here, I guess," Hannah mumbled.

Well apparently not everyone hated the smell. It was earthy, so I guess maybe it would appeal to some people.

We followed Ien down the hallway, and he gestured to three doors right across from each other. "Each of the rooms has a shower and fresh clothing. What you're wearing won't work for the ceremony, so you'll need to put on the clothes in the bathroom. When it's over, you're welcome to wear your own things again. You'll be settling into the castles at that point, though."

Great.

Settling into the castles meant we'd be separated, and that meant I'd be stuck with Chaos.

Maybe I'd get lucky and he'd leave me alone.

Something told me I wouldn't, though.

"Where are the fae women?" Elyn asked, voicing the question I'd considered earlier.

Ien looked surprised that she'd asked. "There aren't any, or we would've used them to get home by now. The faeries went extinct thousands of years ago."

We all stared at him like he was insane.

"Then how are fae born?" Hannah broke the silence.

"They aren't. Fae live until we're killed, and when we die, we reform in the center of Avalon. There's no birth, and death isn't permanent the way it is on your planet."

... WHAT?

"Is death permanent for you here?" Elyn checked.

"No. We're reborn at the center of Avalon Island."

I guess that was what they called this place; Avalon Island. It fit.

But it wasn't very creative, considering they'd come from a place called Avalon.

Ien opened one of the doors and gestured for Elyn to go in. "Please get ready quickly. We need to move forward with the power transfer ceremony, so we can progress toward getting home."

Elyn stood in the doorway of the room Ien had opened for her, hesitating. "Will the power transfer hurt us?"

"We don't know. Something like this has never been attempted before." He shrugged. "It shouldn't be painful, based on what we do know, but there's no way to be sure."

With a nod, Elyn slipped into her room and closed the door.

Ien led Hannah to the door beside Elyn's, and when she was secured inside, led me across the hallway.

He paused before opening the room for me, his expression hesitant. "I apologize for King Auden's behavior. There is much more water on your Earth than Avalon, and as the water is his element, he's much stronger here—and much less controlled because of it. Even more than the rest of us, he looks forward to returning home."

"Great." I didn't bother smiling at him.

Regardless of the king's power-level or how much he was struggling, it didn't take much effort to be a decent person or treat other people decently.

Or *not kill them*.

Ien added, "Just don't—"

I opened the door, interrupting his attempt at getting me to feel compassion for the jerk of a king. "Better get ready." I stepped inside.

Ien got the message. At least the fae weren't completely oblivious. "We'll be back for you in an hour. I know women need much time to prepare, but I hope that will suffice."

"Mmhmm." I shut the door in his face, turning my back to it and sagging against the thick, warm rock that kept the fae out.

Now that I knew why they had taken us, I didn't need to be as afraid of them.

They needed us.

They were going to give us their power—which sounded

like a crappy idea, based on what their power had done to our world.

They had no intentions of using or abusing us for anything other than a portal back to Avalon... assuming Ien's word could be trusted.

Which was doubtful, because he was fae.

But there was usually some truth to every good lie, wasn't there? So at least some of what he said was most-likely true.

With a tired sigh, I tilted my head back against the rock and closed my eyes. The air really, really stank of dirt, but there were far bigger issues to worry about.

I could still try to escape if I wanted. I could make a run for it—or a swim for it, I guess.

But again... someone had to be the sacrifice.

Someone had to give up their life to save the world.

So why not me?

With society crushed and crumbling, my future as a pianist was probably over. My job at the diner was toast, too. And on top of that, I didn't have any family.

By staying with the fae, I could save someone else from this crappy fate. I'd have to turn into a fae—or a faery, I guess —and deal with stuff relating to that, but it would be worth it.

At least, it would be worth it for our world.

With a tired sigh as I gave up all hope of escaping this crappy fate, I opened my eyes again.

They'd given us an hour.

An hour was enough time to shower, change, and take at

least a forty-minute nap, if I could actually sleep. The sleep wasn't likely, but it was a possibility.

For once, I was grateful for the media's ridiculous portrayal of women needing hours upon hours just to prepare for the day. I could count on one hand the number of times it had taken me more than ten minutes to get ready. Usually, it was more like five—tugging a brush through my hair, swiping mascara on my lashes (when I remembered) and throwing on clean underwear and semi-clean pants.

But because I didn't know what their ceremony would be like and if my fifth-day hair would affect it, I figured I'd scrub myself clean with fae soap before attempting a nap.

I checked out the room first. It was pretty big, but bare other than a king-sized bed and a dresser. There were no decorations, and the floor and walls were made of the same bland brown stone.

The bathroom was much the same, though there was a simple shower inside it with normal human plumbing.

I glanced at the pile of clean, white clothing folded neatly beside the sink. Though I wanted to check it out, I was a little paranoid that touching it would screw up the sketchy ceremony I was going to be a part of. So I left it, and got in the shower.

There was a brand new bar of soap inside, and nothing else. I sniffed it suspiciously, and frowned at the smell. It was light, but fresh, and didn't smell like any one thing in particular. I'd never smelled anything quite like it, but it was nice.

Without any shampoo in sight, I just went ahead and

lathered some of the nice-smelling soap in my hands and scrubbed my head with it.

I got out a few minutes later, drying off with an ultra-soft towel I found hanging on the wall.

When I was dry, I pulled the new clothing off the countertop, and my eyes shot upward. I would've expected a society without women to put us in skimpy or sheer clothes that would show our bodies—either on purpose or by accident—but what I found was neither.

There was a soft white sports bra, a pair of boxer shorts made out of the same material, and a simple white tank-dress to go over the top. It wasn't see-through or low-cut, and there was no slit in the bottom portion.

I didn't much like dresses, but I could appreciate that we wouldn't be naked in front of however many fae dudes would be at this power-transfer ceremony. If it was dresses or full-on nudity, I'd go for a dress in a heartbeat.

I pulled on the bra and shorts and then tugged the comb I'd found on the counter through my hair. The fae soap had left it surprisingly smooth.

With my hair detangled, I carried the dress out to the bedroom area and tossed it over the end of the bed before climbing onto the mattress.

I doubted I'd be able to nap, but I'd try.

Slipping under the covers, I was surprised by the softness of the sheets. They were either fae-made, or really damned expensive. Since the fae had only been on Earth for a few weeks, I was guessing the latter.

My head hit the pillow, and I stared up at the ceiling. The

bedroom's light was off but the bathroom's was on; I wasn't used to sleeping in complete darkness.

Rather than resting, my mind went back to my home.

My piano.

My chest suddenly felt very tight.

I'd been raised by my grandparents until my grandma died when I was ten. Then, it had just been me and Grandpa. He'd tried to teach me that it was okay to cry, but I just preferred to pour my emotions into my music rather than let them overwhelm me.

Without my piano, or my home, or... anything else but my memories, really, I was lost.

I had been for a while, if I was honest.

But at least I had my gun, assuming whatever fae who had carried it off the boat didn't go through my bag and did eventually give it back.

A rapid knock at the door had me sitting up.

It swung open slightly, and Elyn peeked inside. "Noa?"

"Yeah, come in," I slid out from under the blankets.

Elyn and Hannah slipped inside, closing the door quietly behind themselves. They were both wearing the same thing I was, though they'd put the dresses on and mine was still hanging over the end of the bed.

"Are there any fae guarding the hallway?" I checked.

"One at each end," Hannah confirmed. "They didn't seem to have a problem with us coming over here, though."

That fit with what they'd said about needing us. They wanted us to open a portal—and that was it.

But I wasn't stupid; if we opened a portal, they'd probably drag us through it with them.

"If they're telling the truth, this is probably the best-case scenario for the rest of our planet," I admitted. "Three orphan girls go to the fae world, leaving earth fae-free so it can heal."

"And any bookworm's dream," Hannah added wistfully. "Gorgeous, massive fae men whisking us away from our sad lives. It sounds more romantic in the books than it feels in real life, though."

I could imagine.

Not much was romantic about getting ripped suddenly away from everything you knew and loved, after all.

"So, you don't think we should try to escape?" Elyn asked Hannah.

She shook her head. "No. If we leave, they'll either find us, kill us, or pick some other average women."

Elyn looked at me. "What about you, Noa?"

I'd reached the same conclusion as Hannah already. "Yeah, I don't see a purpose to leaving. Even if we managed to get back home, the government would probably come looking for us. And the world's fallen apart anyway, so what's the point?"

My whole life had revolved around my YouTube channel before the fae appeared. I rewrote popular songs and recorded covers of myself playing them on the piano at night after work, and while I wasn't anywhere near one of the top-dogs on the video site, my channel had been growing slowly but surely.

After the fae had come and their disasters had stopped, YouTube was still up and running, but no one was on the internet anymore. Instead, they were with their family or friends, trying to figure out how to cope with the utter hell that had ravaged our world.

Elyn nodded. "I agree. But even if we don't make a run for it, I think we need a plan. We're the only humans here, and the only women... we need to work together."

Truthfully, I was the kind of person who let other people make the plans when it came to social stuff. I was focused on one thing: my music. With everything else, I just tried to go with the flow and survive whatever life threw at me.

Then again, life had never thrown an angry blond fae dude at me before. Maybe it was time to adapt.

"I'm in," Hannah agreed.

"Me too." I bobbed my head.

"Are you guys freaked out about becoming fae?" Hannah changed the subject.

Freaked out? That was an understatement. "Dude, yes."

"Isn't it suspicious that they wiped out all the faery chicks?" Elyn checked. "I feel like we need more of an explanation about that. Are we going to be hunted once we get them back home? Or is their land poisonous to women or something?"

I grimaced. "We'll have to ask Ien. He seems like the least-difficult one."

"I'm just glad I'm not saddled with Chaos," Elyn muttered, shooting me an apologetic frown. I almost corrected her that Ien said his real name was Auden, but there was no point to it. I didn't know him, and he did seem to deserve the nickname. "He seems like a real asshole."

"Yeah, I'm sorry," Hannah agreed.

I waved it off. "It's fine. I can handle him."

Maybe it was a lie, but I hoped it was true. I really didn't want to get murdered by the sea king.

CHAPTER 4

WE SPENT another half an hour talking about our options —which were slim—and what we could do if one of the kings stepped out of line and tried to hurt us—which wasn't much. I hadn't really had any female friends since elementary school, so it was weird to be talking with Elyn and Hannah like we were best buds, but it was necessary. We were all each other had for the time-being, whether we liked it or not.

There was a polite knock on the door, and our conversation cut off instantly.

We all exchanged looks, and I finally got up and crossed the room, tugging my dress on before going to the door. Pulling it open, I found myself face to face with Ien.

"The kings are ready," he said, once again cheerful.

I glanced over my shoulder, my eyes meeting those of the other women. They crossed the room, all three of us barefoot and in our sacrificial-white dresses.

"You're not going to kill us, right?" Elyn asked, suddenly.

I mean, it was a valid question.

Ien frowned. "Of course not. We need you to get back to Avalon."

"I mean after you're back in Avalon," she clarified.

Understanding dawned in his eyes. "Not unless it's required."

Required?

Right.

What a terrible, uninspiring answer.

We followed him out of the castle, and back down to the gazebo.

"We're doing this near the ocean, to make things easier for the sea king," he explained, as we walked through the gazebo and down toward the ocean.

I was pretty sure Ien had mentioned Chaos, AKA Auden, AKA the blond angry one, being the sea king. And I was pretty sure he'd said Kalus was the earth king. What did that make Merzo? I had a few guesses, but nothing concrete.

The kings were waiting on the beach, shirtless this time. Somehow, they managed to be even more intimidating while half-naked.

Merzo, the quieter redheaded king, had tattoos all over his torso and wrapping around his shoulders, but neither of the other kings had a shred of ink that I could see.

We approached the group, and the redheaded kings strode over to the sides of the women they'd picked.

Auden just glared at me from across the beach.

I gave him a thumbs-up just to annoy him further, and his strange eyes seemed to darken.

"We'll start with Hannah and Kalus," Ien said.

His cheerfulness was really getting old, though it was still preferable to the hatred coming from the sea king.

"How does this work?" Hannah asked.

"Kalus," Ien gestured to the earth king.

Kalus pulled a folding pocket knife out of his pants, clicking the button to open it up. It looked similar to one from the bucket of pocket-knives I inherited from my grandpa when he died; I had a handful of them in my suitcase, wherever it had gone.

"We'll exchange my people's vows, sealing our marriage, and then you'll cut into my skin with this. While I bleed, you'll put your hand on my wound, and some of my magic will soak into you as it leaves me. It'll heal quickly."

"What? Why?" She looked nauseous.

What kind of screwed-up world did these fae come from?

Hannah was suddenly very, very pale. "I can't cut you."

"Sure you can." He tried to hand her the knife.

She grew a bit green. "I really can't."

"I'll go first," I interrupted her before she could vomit, flinging a hand toward the sea king. "I can't wait to cut into this asshole."

It was a lie; I didn't like harming things any more than Hannah seemed to. But I'd gone fishing with my grandpa almost every weekend for ten and a half years. Once or twice a year he would catch something he wanted to eat, and I'd help him filet the fish. So, I wasn't new to cutting living shit.

I'd always hated doing it, but maybe if she had a little

time to wrap her mind around what she'd need to do, she wouldn't puke.

The ocean crashed a bit closer to us, and the tide rolled over our feet for the first time since we'd been standing there. I ignored the water's weight as it tugged on the hem of my dress, staring at Auden with a bit of a challenge in my eyes.

"Fine." Auden bit the word out, striding over to me. He shoved a knife at me, and I took it from his hand much more casually than he probably expected.

"What am I supposed to say?" I looked at Ien, assuming Auden was going to make it harder than it needed to be.

"Auden will speak the vow of the sea fae in our language. As he binds himself to you, your mind should adapt to the language so you can translate it yourself," he explained.

My eyebrows lifted; that sounded crazy.

But whatever, I guess.

"Right hand," Auden grunted at me.

I moved the knife to my left and held it out. His gigantic hand engulfed mine, and those eerie silver eyes glared down at me.

His lips opened, and the most beautiful words I'd ever heard came from him.

"Illete o retula. Ollete a povena. Errete y—" something that felt like a flash of heat in my chest flared, and my knife-holding hand reached up to it as Auden's words became not English, but understandable. I listened until he'd finished, and then, after a glance at Ien and an encouraging nod, repeated the words back.

"From shore to shore, from wave to wave, my vow to you

will never break. Steady as the sea, strong as the current, in life and death I am yours to take."

The warmth in my chest became a blazing fire that took my breath away. My heart beat rapidly, and Auden grabbed my wrist holding the knife.

I was afraid for all of half a second—because that was when he used my hand to slice a slanted cut across the middle of his forearm.

I dropped the knife immediately, like it was going to burn me.

He caught it, and deftly wiped the blade over my bicep before folding it and tucking it into his pocket, all while glaring at me.

Knowing it was what I was supposed to do, I pressed my hand to the cut and held tightly to his muscley forearm.

The wound closed up quickly, and the blood stopped spilling. It was all over my hand, but none had dripped to the sand or anything. The ocean was moving a mile a minute behind us though, churning and spinning like there was a tornado beneath its surface.

"What was that?" I asked him, pulling a hand away to rub my chest. Blood smeared over my skin, but I didn't care. It was over, at least.

"A fae marriage. They're unbreakable." He stepped away from me as my jaw fell open.

"Unbreakable?" I had been hoping for an eventual divorce, after whatever I did to help them get back to Avalon. Even if I was stuck there, I didn't want to get stuck in a loveless arranged marriage.

He ignored my question, spinning on his heels and walking back into the ocean.

It churned faster as he walked in deeper and deeper until it swallowed him whole.

I watched with my mouth hanging open, once again a damned fish.

Great.

Just freakin' great.

Ien turned back to Hannah. "Ready?" his voice was far too cheerful.

She was even paler than before, and sticky with sweat. "No."

"You'll feel better when it's over. The magic will bring color back to your cheeks—and hair."

What?

"Your hair." Elyn gestured to her boob, and I glanced down at my chest.

I grabbed a piece of hair, my eyes narrowing when I found it at least two inches longer than it had been five minutes ago. And, it was... lighter? Only a shade or two, but there was enough of a difference to notice it.

"Faeries had a very particular appearance," Ien offered. "Long hair, pointed ears, tall, athletic figures. The magic may change how you look. And because it doesn't belong to you, it may alter your appearance to look more like its owner.

Sickness turned my stomach.

"I'm going to turn into a *man*?"

People could do whatever they wanted, and change their bodies however they felt best suited them. I didn't judge. But having my body changed for me without permission or agreement? Yeah, I wasn't cool with that.

"No, no. Fae and faery magic affect coloring, and nothing else."

Phew.

"So she's going to turn blonde? And her eyes will go that same whitish color?" Elyn wondered.

"Precisely."

"I'm going to be a ginger?" Hannah asked, her expression one of disbelief as she glanced at the hair on the man beside her. It was messy and spiked up, but very, very red.

"Yup. Come on." Kalus grabbed Hannah's right hand, sticking the knife in her left.

He spoke a few words in the fae language. I could understand them as if he was speaking them in English, thanks to whatever had happened when Auden and I were connected.

Married.

Wow, I freakin' hated the idea of that.

The earth vow was similar to the sea one, but with peaks and plains instead of waves and shore, along with other earth terminology.

Kalus helped Hannah cut his skin, the same way Auden had helped me, though Kalus was a little gentler about it. Hannah dry-heaved while she held his bleeding arm, but luckily, nothing came up.

When the wound was healed and he told her she could let go, she scrambled backward and dropped to her hands and knees on the sand, gagging while she struggled to breathe.

"Good work." He patted her on the back, and then left.

But unlike Auden, he didn't walk into the ocean—he disappeared into the trees.

The process repeated with Elyn and Merzo, though she wasn't nearly as sick about it as Hannah, and then Merzo left too.

But he didn't leave alone—he wrapped an arm around Elyn and shot up into the air.

Hannah and I gawked after them as they disappeared into the massively-tall mountains, headed up toward the top. I hoped there was a house up there or something; I doubted she would survive any better than I would on top of a mountain.

And I wouldn't survive, so... yeah.

"He can fly?" Hannah breathed.

"She will too, when she possesses enough of his magic," Ien nodded. "Now, we'd better get you two back to your husbands' houses before the bonds settle in."

What did that mean? Why weren't they already settled?

Hannah voiced the question I thought, but Ien ignored her.

"Ah, just in time," he said in a voice still so freakin' cheerful that I wanted to strangle him.

The green-haired fae I'd spent an unfortunate amount of time with appeared, walking out of the ocean. He was dripping wet, but otherwise didn't seem fazed by the choppy water he'd emerged from.

"Chaos sent me to collect his wife," Green-Hair announced.

"Perfect. We'll meet up again later," Ien said, nodding toward Green-Hair.

Green-Hair came toward me, and I took a step back. "Don't go picking me up again," I warned. "I'm not going for a swim."

"Unless you can fly, you're not going to have a choice," Green-Hair growled. "You've got to swim to our castle."

"Is it underwater?" My eyebrows lifted high.

He barked out a laugh. "No. Come on."

I glanced backward at Hannah one last time. She gave me a forced smile, which I returned, before I trudged out onto the sand.

My dress grew heavier with water as I waded in deeper. I wasn't a great swimmer in the first place, so I knew the clothing was going to make me struggle if I didn't remove it.

Pulling the dress over my head, I tossed it to the green-haired fae before glancing down at my tits. I'd assumed the white fabric would be see-through when wet, but much to my surprise, it wasn't.

Phew.

With my naked bits good and covered, I dove out into the water. The pull on my hair was unnaturally strong, given that my hair was growing unnaturally longer, but I had bigger problems.

Namely, keeping up with Green-Hair.

Chapter 5

Despite our long swim, when we finally reached the island that held Auden's castle, I didn't feel tired. I felt...rejuvenated.

It was an odd sensation, but one I liked. Who didn't like feeling rejuvenated?

I wrung my hair out as I waded out of the water, my feet moving carefully over the soft, squishy sand beneath my toes. I didn't want to step on anything sharp, after all.

I glanced at my hair as I let go of it, and forced myself to keep breathing evenly when I noticed that it was even lighter —it was officially, definitely blonde now. Not as light as Auden's, but getting there. And it had grown long enough to cover my boobs, already, which was weird and unnatural all on its own.

I guess the sea king's magic was settling in, somehow. Changing me.

My eyes skimmed the castle. The place was massive, and

built Spanish-style as a sprawling, one-story building that stretched a long way to both my right and my left. The warm-toned white walls with the reddish-orange roof, along with the curves and arches, were breathtaking.

It didn't even almost resemble a castle from a storybook, but if they wanted to call it that, I didn't care.

We walked inside the open doors at the front of the building, and then walked straight through another set of doors, and found ourselves in some kind of a courtyard.

Green grass and plants of all colors decorated the courtyard, which was framed by the large building. From within, I saw dozens of doors, stretching as far as I could see and curving through the space.

"How did you build this so fast?" I wondered.

He ignored the question, as if I hadn't asked it at all.

I felt eyes on me, and heard a few doors open and close before more fae began to appear in the courtyard, leaving their homes and stepping out to stare at me.

"A faery," someone whispered.

I opened my mouth to announce that I wasn't a faery, and then stopped.

Maybe I kind of *was* a faery.

Or at least, kind of was becoming one.

Wow, that was freaky to think about.

My mouth closed.

Green-Hair walked me through the courtyard. We wove around and through a few different buildings; the place was freakin' massive.

Finally, we found Auden's portion of the castle. It was on

the beach—even more so than the rest of the place—and was its own building entirely, separate from everyone else's.

Was the castle really his if he didn't even live inside it? Hard to say.

Green-Hair walked me up to the door, but stopped on the small patio. "This is where I leave you." He gestured toward the door. "Best not to anger the king."

"Isn't he always angry?" I lifted an eyebrow.

Every time I'd seen him, he looked pissed.

He ignored me again.

"I'm right here, asshole," I snapped at the fae.

Probably shouldn't have done that, but I was on a roll when it came to doing things I shouldn't. Why not keep it going?

"I owe you nothing. You humans and your temporary lives are nothing compared to our immortal souls," he sneered. "Just a touch of our magic, and look at you— changing so much, in such a short period of time. We're the best thing that's ever happened to this pitiful plane—"

I couldn't help myself—I stepped toward him, and slugged him in the face. My grandpa had taught me how to throw a punch, but shit, it still hurt.

I shook out my hand as I stepped back.

The fae spun me around and shoved me into the door, and my back collided with the thick wood hard enough to knock the breath out of me and make my head ache.

His glare was hot and angry. "You're going to regret that."

Yeah, probably.

But at that point, I pretty much regretted all of the choices that had led to me becoming a sacrificial, average human, so what was one more regret on top of that?

His fist flew toward my face, and I barely had time to blink, let alone—

A large figure caught Green-Hair's fist.

"What the wist are you doing?" the hulking fae snarled at Green-Hair, shoving him backward. "Do you know what the punishment was for attacking a queen, Joge? For hurting a man's *kompel*? A decade hanging from the wilder tree, with only enough food to keep you alive."

I stared, wide-eyed, at Auden's back.

I'd forgotten how massive the blond fae was in the thirty minutes we'd been apart.

The king shoved Green-Hair, AKΛ Joge, backward again, and stalked the man toward the ocean.

"You're not really married," Joge argued. "And she punched me."

Auden snarled back, "There's no way to reverse a marriage, so yes, this female is mine. And I don't give a wist whether or not we're actually together—you're going to suffer far more than she does if you ever so much as touch her again."

Joge muttered something I couldn't hear, and a wave rose up. It ripped him out into the ocean, and I stared after him with my lips rounded once again.

Auden stormed past me, ripping the door open and violently gesturing me inside.

I eyed him uncertainly. "I'm good out here."

"Get inside *now*," he growled in the fae language.

"Fine." I stepped past him, never taking my narrowed eyes off him. He was dangerous, and even though he'd protected me, he still seemed like a loose cannon.

"Your things are in your room. Don't leave," he barked, and then disappeared into a bedroom off to my left.

When he was gone, I looked around the house. It didn't hold much. Just a kitchen, and a couch in the living area—no dining table, even.

The bathroom was just a shower without a curtain in it, sitting beside a toilet.

I caught a glimpse of my reflection in the mirror and ended up standing there, staring at myself for far too long.

It was the strangest thing.

The color was leaving my eyes and hair, while my hair was growing longer. The shape of my body was even changing, growing taller, and slimming in some places while thickening in others.

And, staring in that mirror, I realized I'd probably miss the *averageness* of the way I was before, eventually.

Slipping out of the bathroom, I headed to the only other room in the house. I knew that had to be my bedroom, and according to Auden, my things were in there.

I looked forward to putting on my own clothes.

And maybe, getting some sleep.

Though I doubted I'd be able to sleep in the same house as Auden. He had protected me from the other fae, but I wasn't under the impression that it had meant anything.

Plenty of abusers would protect their families from someone, just to go home and hurt them themselves.

I found my bedroom and looked around. It was even emptier than the one I'd borrowed back at the earth castle; all it held was a bed. It was a large one, at least—but then the fae were large people, so I imagined they didn't have any interest in small furniture.

My suitcase sat on my bed, looking unopened.

My body tensed as the moment of truth arose; had they found my gun?

I unzipped my suitcase, flopping it open. Everything looked a bit mixed-up, but it had been on a plane, and then on a boat, so that didn't really mean anything.

My fingers worked through the items in the bag, and my heartbeat picked up when my hand wrapped around the gun.

It was still mine.

I wasn't entirely unprotected.

Tucking it beneath the mattress on my bed, I went back to my bag and found the rest of my tools, weapons, and other crap that had been either mine, my grandma's, or my grandpa's.

I expected I'd need to take a shower after the long swim, but I didn't feel dirty.

Surprisingly enough, the saltwater dried on my skin didn't make my skin feel dry. I clearly remembered my skin feeling stiff and inflamed when I'd gone to the beach on the one and only vacation my grandpa and I had ever taken. It was my senior trip, right after I graduated. Just me and him sitting on the beach, drinking beer and talking about every-thing and nothing for days on end. It had been one of the best weeks of my life.

I grabbed my clothes and headed to the shower anyway though; I hated it when my skin got dry, and it always made me break out.

After closing my suitcase, I slipped into the bathroom. I locked the door, stripped, and then double-checked that it was locked because my paranoia on Avalon Island was real. When I was double-sure the lock was in place, I stepped into the shower.

Usually I liked hot showers, but the hot water didn't feel warm at all. I fiddled with the temperature, trying to make it hotter, but even the cold didn't seem to work.

It was odd; I'd never taken a shower when the tempera-ture was a constant lukewarm.

It wasn't very pleasant though, so I scrubbed clean with what looked like an unused bar of soap. Water spilled every-where thanks to the missing shower curtain, but since Auden was the one who didn't have a shower curtain, I figured the soaking-wet towels after I was done cleaning up would be his problem.

I showered quickly, then spent ten minutes mopping up the floor. My hair was dry by the time I was done cleaning the floor—something that had never happened in my life.

What the hell had Auden's magic done to me?

Shaking my head in disbelief, I pulled on clean under-wear along with some jean cutoffs and another faded old Tom's Garage shirt. I still didn't feel cold... or hot, either.

Padding out to the kitchen, I opened the fridge. It was nice, but simple; nothing fancy, just like the rest of Auden's house. And I liked that, even if I didn't really want to admit it.

"Nothin' but shelves," I drawled at the empty fridge.

What did he eat? There weren't even any condiments or anything.

I really didn't want to talk to the asshole I'd managed to get myself *married* to—thank you, last pick in the schoolyard —but I was hungry. And I hated being hungry.

The only thing that waiting would achieve was making me hungrier. Eventually, I'd have to confront Auden so he could realize that even *average human women* needed to eat.

With an inward sigh, I walked to the door Auden had disappeared inside.

My fist rapped the wood. "Auden?" I paused, waiting for an answer.

No response.

I knocked again, harder. "Chaos?"

I didn't much like the nickname; seemed a bit ridiculous to me. But whatever. Maybe that was what he preferred to answer to.

No answer, again.

Maybe he just wasn't there.

"I'm opening the door if I don't hear from you in ten seconds," I called out.

No response, again.

With an outward sigh, that time, I twisted the doorknob and opened the door.

My head peeked inside at a bedroom just as plain and nondescript as mine. He had the same one piece of furniture as me, and the same plain white bedspread over the bed, even. It didn't look slept in, and there were no clothes on the floor or anything.

"I should've heard you leave," I remarked, walking into the room and checking things out.

He didn't have a bathroom in there; guess we were sharing the other one. He did have a small closet though, and all I saw in there was a row of six of the exact same pair of jeans and seven of the exact same white t-shirt.

"Good call on the white," I remarked to the closet, as if Auden was inside. "You'd definitely look like one of those 'dark ones' from fantasy movies and TV shows if you wore black."

Turning back to the room, I looked around the empty space again.

This time, my eyes landed on an open window.

"Aha. So that's why I didn't hear you."

I left the room, closing the door behind me so he wouldn't know I'd snooped around his absolutely boring and empty bedroom.

He'd told me not to leave... but I was hungry, and *he* had left.

So, guess I was ignoring that command. Husbands shouldn't be able to command their wives anyway though, right?

I headed out through the front door, going back into the main castle area. Hearing some noise from the center of one of the many sprawling courtyards, I wove through grass sections and openings between buildings until I found the source of the commotion.

Stopping on the edge of the space when I found it, I looked over a cafeteria of sorts, with picnic tables and an outdoor kitchen and everything. The grass beneath the large group of fae looked stunningly healthy, and it was even greener than the perfect lawn my grandpa had kept up with until he'd hired someone else to do it when he was no longer able.

And well, at least I'd found the food.

There were eyes on me. Lots of eyes.

That wasn't surprising though, since I was the only creature with boobs on their whole island.

I ignored the stares, walking over to the line of fae holding plates and waiting for food. Auden didn't appear to be among the group, which was good. I didn't want to have to argue with him in front of his people.

On second thought, did the fae kings even have people, or were their positions just sort of for show, like some of the European countries?

I didn't know, but I'd probably find out eventually.

First, food.

CHAPTER 6

THE FAE in front of me left the line when I joined it.

I shrugged, moving up in the line.

More of the gigantic men peeled away from the group immediately. I continued moving up, growing a bit self-conscious as I approached those serving the food.

Trying to be sneaky, I sniffed my shirt. I'd just had a shower, but maybe I stunk? I'd put on a bra, and I was definitely wearing shorts, so I at least knew I wasn't naked and my nipples weren't pointing up a storm or anything.

The fae serving the first portion of the food bowed deeply toward me. "Queen..." he trailed off, remaining in the bowed position. I may not have been up-to-date on my royalty terms, but I could tell he was asking for my name.

And, yikes.

The last thing I wanted was them *Queen Noa*-ing me every time I saw them.

"Noa. Just Noa." I held out my plate, wiggling it around.

"Nothing special here, no need to bow. I just want some potatoes."

The fae's expression was a bit shocked, but he slapped a gigantic scoop of mashed potatoes on my plate. They looked like the homemade stuff, with bits of potato and skin inside… yum.

I nodded my approval and gave him a thumbs-up with the hand that wasn't holding the plate. "Thanks." I moved forward.

The next fae started to bow too.

"I'm going to stop you right there, bud. I'm only here because I have to be, and I really just want to get this over with, so just stick some food on my plate and be done with it."

The fae stopped his bow halfway, straightening and plopping some corn on my plate.

"Thanks." I nodded at him too before continuing.

The rest of the fae serving the food wisely decided not to bow, but they gave me way more food than I could ever eat.

I wasn't going to complain about that, though, since Auden's fridge was empty and all.

My plate was a legitimate mountain when I walked away from the food line, my eyes scanning the crowd.

No one was eating; they were all just staring at me.

I considered pulling Viola's move from *She's the Man* and just flashing my tits at all of them to get the awkwardness over with, but figured that probably wasn't the best introduction.

With another inward sigh, I looked around at all of the tables.

Yeah, it was definitely feeling like high school all over again.

There were no empty tables, so I was going to have to join one. Or sit on my ass on the grass. But something about being on the ground while a hundred gigantic fae towered over me, stronger in every single way, didn't feel right to me.

My eyes traced over the empty seats. I didn't know if fae separated themselves in their cafeteria like high school did. They were all so gorgeous it was hard to decide if they were divided by populars, losers, warriors, clothing-makers, and etc.

The shortest fae I could see had an empty seat next to him, so I just walked over there. Maybe his shortness compared to the others would've put him on the outside like I was.

As soon as I sat down, he and the other four fae at the table all got up with their plates and walked away.

"Wow. Clearly, I am desirable company," I muttered, digging my fork into the potato mountain.

The food was so good I could've cried.

Instead, I just shoveled it in like I was a drowning person and the food was air.

The fae ignored me while I ate, and the volume of the cafeteria never picked back up to anywhere near what it had been. If they wanted to let me ruin their fun, that was fine; it was their choice to make. I was busy becoming a food addict, anyway, so I didn't really care.

When I was full, I carried my plate over to the large sink a few fae were scrubbing dishes at, and handed it over with a smile. "Thanks, guys."

Giving them a quick salute, I headed back toward Auden's part of the castle.

The noise picked back up, louder than it had been, as soon as I was gone. My lips twisted in a grimace; they were definitely all gossiping about me. I'd been better friends with guys than other girls my whole life, so I knew the idea that men didn't gossip like women was bullshit. They just did it a bit differently.

I was walking down the beach, toward the house, when Auden strode out of the ocean. He looked like some kind of angry drowned angel with that shock of white-blond hair on his head, and the fury in his odd eyes.

"I told you not to leave," he growled at me.

I shrugged. "I was hungry."

He could be as much of a dick as he wanted; I wasn't going to apologize for eating when I was hungry. I may have been a human sacrifice, but I refused to be a damned prisoner.

His anger grew. "I sent one of my fae to get you groceries."

"They were too slow. And groceries require cooking; you have a cafeteria full of incredible food in there." I gestured behind me.

"Incredible food, and dangerous fae. Many of which will want to either bed you or kill you for what you are to me."

Yikes. "Well, none of them tried anything today."

He ignored that fact. "If you insist on leaving again, I'll have to assign you a guard. And I'd *pity* any man forced to follow you around all day."

I scoffed. "*I* pity the man who has to do everything you say. Good thing I'm not him; as I've proved, I'm a terrible listener."

He stepped past me and threw the door open. "Clearly we need to work on that."

"Good luck with that, *Chaos*." I followed him in, letting the door shut hard behind us.

We went to our individual rooms, and both of our doors slammed.

I ENTERTAINED myself on my phone for a few hours, up until my battery died. Though I didn't have phone service, I had a few games on there that didn't require the internet.

Digging through my suitcase for the charger, I pulled it out and looked for an outlet. There wasn't one anywhere in the room, so I headed out to the living room to search there.

When I went out, I found Auden cooking at the stove, shirtless and absolutely way too freakin' attractive, especially from behind... because from behind, I didn't have to see him glaring at me.

The cut on his arm had healed strangely, I realized—the scar looked silverish and shimmery.

My gaze went up to his hair, my mind going back to his eyes.

The scar's coloring was somewhere between the two of

them... was that because of the magic that had spilled out of it?

"What are you doing?" he asked, without turning around.

"Trying to find a power outlet," I called.

And checking you out, I added mentally.

But I wasn't saying that out loud.

"There are no power outlets. Human technology and electricity make our magic unpredictable."

"Then why do you have a kitchen? And lights?" I countered.

He shot me a look that told me he thought I was a moron. "Ien saw that we'd have to marry humans on the first day we arrived here, and we built our temporary homes accordingly."

Ah. "Why did you come here, though? Seems a bit counterintuitive to come here and destroy our world all while trying to get home."

"We didn't come by choice." His irritation sounded like it had grown to an even higher level, somehow.

"I have a hard time believing someone sent *you* here by force."

"I have a hard time caring about what you believe."

Ouch.

Fair, though.

"Well, on that loving note, I'm going to bed," I announced, taking my now-useless phone with me.

Maybe one of the other human women would talk one

of the less-difficult kings into letting her have a power outlet, and I could talk her into letting me use it.

Closing and locking the door behind me, I tossed my phone onto my suitcase and slipped into bed.

I SLEPT straight through the morning, waking up to a jerk banging on my door.

"Get up, November," Auden barked. "I told you, we're doing the transfer at noon."

"I don't have a clock," I yelled back, groggy. "Some dick wouldn't let me charge my phone."

"Get dressed and out here in five minutes or I'll drag your naked ass to the beach myself."

"I'm flipping you off through the door," I shot back, stumbling toward it. I was still wearing the day before's clothes, but they were fresh-ish. Or at least, not smelly yet.

"So terrifying," the king drawled as I yanked the door open, pushing hair out of my eyes.

Something caught on my jeans, and I glanced down. Horror struck me.

Shoving past the jerk in the doorway, I stepped into the bathroom and stared at myself in the mirror.

Mouth hanging open like a fish yet again, I just... stared.

My hair fell to my ass in neat waves. It was crazy thick, and the exact same color as Auden's. All of the brown had leeched from my eyes, leaving them the silvery-white that my new *husband's* were.

"Crap." I nearly choked on my own spit just saying the

word. "What am I supposed to do with a hundred pounds of *hair*?"

"Sell it." He was being sarcastic, but I was ignoring the sarcasm.

"If cutting it works, I definitely will."

"Of course it wouldn't work; your hair would just grow back, like any other body part. You're a faery now."

"I'm a freakin' alien, now," I snapped back, gesturing at myself in the mirror.

"If you think that's bad, look at these." Auden grabbed my hair, lifting it so I could see the top of my right ear.

The blood drained from my face when I saw the point where there should've been an arch.

Elf ears. Faery ears. I had pointy elf/faery ears.

I didn't even manage to get a word out when I choked on air, that time.

"We're going to be late," he grumbled. "Stop staring at yourself; we need to go."

"My entire body is changing because of your magic. I deserve at least three minutes to stare at myself," I shot back.

Wisely, he didn't respond to that.

"Do I need to wear a dress again?" I finally checked, done freaking out about my appearance. The long hair was obnoxious and the body-change was insane, but I was still me. At least, on the inside.

"No. That was for the wedding ceremony." The words were surprisingly civil for a man who called himself Chaos.

"Right. Great."

I followed him out the door.

He headed straight into the water. I followed him in until the water met my knees, but hesitated there. I still had on jean cutoffs and a t-shirt, which weren't exactly good swimming clothes. Talk about chafing.

He glanced back at me.

"I didn't know this fae-wife gig would require swimming. I'm going to need a few swimsuits," I warned him, wading back out of the water.

Auden's response was to glare at me, of course. Because that made sense, given I was the one who'd been sacrificed to him, and not the other way around.

"What are you doing?" he growled as I unbuttoned my shorts.

"What does it look like I'm doing? Stripping, obviously." I grabbed my shorts off the sand and tossed them up toward the house just in case the tide came up higher, then tugged my shirt over my head. I hadn't been comfortable enough in Auden's house to sleep without a bra, so my trusty electric-purple t-shirt bra was on display. I didn't much like the color, but she'd been twenty bucks cheaper than her other-colored sisters during a bra sale a couple years ago and yes, I was that cheap. "Come on, it's a free show. Human guys pay to watch shit like this."

I waded back into the water, and noticed Auden's typical angry face even tighter than usual. "You let human men pay you to take your clothes off?"

I rolled my eyes. "No, I don't. But some people do, and since it's their body, they get to do whatever they want with it. Keep whatever misogynistic thoughts you have about that to yourself."

The water moved angrily around us at my words. I wasn't sure what that meant or why, but I assumed Auden was doing it himself, on purpose.

"Keep up." He bit the words out before diving into the water.

"How am I supposed to keep up with you if I can't see you?" I threw my hands out at my sides. My stomach growled, and I itched to go back the fae cafeteria place, but didn't want to deal with more of Auden's wrath if I did.

His head popped up a ways in the distance. "Get your ass in the water, November," he yelled.

"It's Noa, asshole!" I yelled back, though I did wade deeper into the water. "And I'm not a damn fish! I can't see you when you vanish under the water!"

Auden didn't yell back again.

Instead, the current whisked me out further into the ocean, its pull too strong for me to fight.

I screamed into the water, barely managing to hold my breath fast enough to avoid a lungful of burning saltwater. Just when I didn't think I could hold my breath any longer, the water ripped me up to the surface and my face met the air.

I sucked in breaths, heart pounding like a jackhammer as I treaded water in an attempt to keep myself from sinking. Surprisingly enough, the treading water part was easy, and something about the feel of the water around me made me calmer.

"What the hell?" I shouted at Auden. I was no professional when it came to ocean waves, tides, and rip currents, but I was pretty sure that hadn't been a natural phenomenon.

And the water made me feel calm*er*, but not *calm*.

"Keep up, or I'll make you." His body turned horizontally, and he started through the water with smooth, deep strokes. Something about the way he moved caught my attention and held it in securely. Those arms, those muscles...

The ocean caught hold of me again, and I closed my eyes and mouth tightly just as I was ripped through the water.

CHAPTER 7

I WAS PANTING when we finally reached the main part of the island.

The ocean tossed me up onto the shore, dropping me on my face, and I groaned into the powdery sand already sticking to my entire front-side.

"Get up," Auden growled.

I lifted my hand, giving him my middle finger and most certainly not getting up.

"Get up, or I'll carry you."

A ride in the arms of a ripped fae didn't sound so bad at the moment. But considering who the ripped fae was, I wasn't on board.

"Touch me without my permission and I'll knee you in the balls so hard your nuts come up through your mouth," I mumbled into the sand.

Very threatening, I know.

"Is she okay?" someone yelled.

My head jerked upward. That had definitely been a feminine voice, and the only women on the island were my new, forced family.

I rubbed sand off my eyes with the back of my arm, then lifted my hand to give the chick a thumbs-up. I didn't know Hannah and Elyn well enough to confidently tell their voices apart yet, but I was fairly sure it was Elyn.

Easing myself up onto my hands and knees, I spit out sand and tried once again to scrub my face clean with the back of my arm.

Nope, that didn't work.

I heard the ocean churning, and then all of the sudden, a wave crashed over me.

I coughed up water as it retreated, but at least the water had taken the sand away with it.

Climbing to my feet, I stumbled and had to grab Auden's arm to remain standing.

Damn, that thing was beefy.

His glaring silvery-white eyes met mine.

Yikes.

I released my hold on him, brushing sand off his bicep hastily before striding over to the waiting fae and humans. Err, fae and... sort of faeries.

My eyes widened at the sight of the women standing on the sand. They were wearing dresses similar to what they'd had on the day before; Elyn's was white, Hannah's was brown. Neither of them had been allowed to go back for any of their stuff, unlike me, so they were stuck with whatever clothing the fae handed them. But like me, they'd *changed*.

Butt-length ruby-red hair fell down their backs in waves, framing faces that looked slightly thinner along with big, jewel-toned eyes. Elyn's were an unnaturally-bright blue, and Hannah's were emerald-green.

"Wow," I said.

What else was there to say? We were all in agreement that becoming faeries was far from ideal, regardless of how it changed us.

"You look like hell," Elyn remarked.

Guess we weren't beating around the bush.

"Thanks. It's a new style I've been trying." I wiped my sandy hands over my bare abdomen. Between my old electric-purple bra and my old black granny panties, I clearly wasn't trying to impress anyone.

"Let's get started," Ien said cheerfully.

I was starting to wonder how the fae resisted strangling his obnoxiously-cheerful face.

"No need for witnesses this time, so just go ahead and start whenever you're ready," he added.

Since the marriages were over with, all there was to do was slice into our *husbands* and bleed 'em.

Yay.

Auden shoved the knife into my hand and tried to take control of it again.

I jerked my arm backward. "I told you not to touch me."

He scowled, but withdrew his hand.

Many unpleasant things could be said about him, but at least he respected that boundary.

"You have to cut deep so it bleeds long enough," Auden growled.

"Fine." I waved him off, grabbing ahold of his wrist and positioning his arm properly. If he was going to have another one of those shimmery cuts on his body, I may as well try to line it up with the other one so it looked more purposeful. It was a shame to mar someone so freakin' gorgeous, but making the markings look like they'd been done on purpose would help.

"So you're allowed to touch me, but I'm not allowed to touch you?" Auden asked, his voice low and—you guessed it—angry.

"If you asked me not to touch you, I wouldn't. But since you haven't, and I'm trying to hold your arm steady so this doesn't look absolutely hideous after it's healed, yes. Now shut up for a minute."

He shut up.

I held his arm still, and as expected, his body tensed just before I sliced through his arm again. My stomach twisted a bit and I dropped the knife, pressing my hand to the cut.

A soft curse escaped him, but the word was a fae one without a translation, and I couldn't make it out exactly.

He caught the knife before it hit the ground, then wiped the blood off the blade onto my arm. The slide of metal over my skin scared me a bit, but the movement was so swift and sure that I knew he wasn't going to hurt me.

"Well, that was awful," I muttered, still holding his arm. The action felt like some kind of ancient sacrificial ritual, but since no one was actually dying, I could try to ignore the strangeness of it.

The cut healed and I finally stepped back, away from Auden.

My bloody hand hung awkwardly at my side, and he tucked his knife back in his pocket before turning and walking away.

I glanced between him and the other ladies.

I really didn't want to go back with him; staying with them would be much preferable. But our connection was still sort of up in the air, and I didn't know how he'd react to me telling him that.

Probably with anger; that was a safe guess.

He stopped at the edge of the water. "November," he barked.

Jerk.

"I told you to call me Noa," I shot back, giving Elyn and Hannah a forced smile before crossing the beach and meeting him at the edge of the water.

"Your name is November."

"And your name is Auden, *Chaos*."

We waded back into the water together.

"Are you going to swim this time, or will I have to drag you again?" He ignored my comment entirely.

Honestly, though, the way he ignored it told me more than any snappy remark would've. He didn't want to acknowledge that people called him Chaos—maybe because he didn't like it, or because it pissed him off?

"Drown me again, you mean?"

He scoffed. "You can breathe water. The only way you'll drown is by letting yourself sink and then refusing to eat for days—in which case you'll be starving, not drowning."

"What?" I gaped at him.

"You resemble a fish." He dove down into the water.

"Yeah, I know," I muttered, shaking my head and diving in after him. I was far from the strong, smooth swimmer Auden was, but I did know how to swim.

He was far ahead of me all the way back to the island, but since I was swimming—and following—he didn't drag me through the water the way he had on the way there.

I should've been exhausted when I finally reached the king's beach house, but like the day before, I just felt *better*. It was the strangest thing.

I would definitely need to try the breathing-underwater thing Auden had told me about, but I'd need to wait until I was back with one or both of the other girls. I didn't trust the fae king to rescue me if I failed at water-breathing; he clearly didn't have many positive feelings toward me.

Back inside the house, my stomach rumbled.

I headed into the kitchen, but heard a strange noise on my way. Stopping, I frowned and listened closer. That time, I didn't hear anything.

But thinking on what I'd heard, I realized it sounded like... a window had opened.

My eyes brightened, and I hurried over to Auden's bedroom door.

My fist rapped the wood. "Auden?"

No answer.

I opened the door and peeked inside, just to be sure he was gone.

Yup; the room was empty.

I did a little butt-shaking victory dance as I went back to my room. After tugging a shirt on, I headed for the front door.

Fae cafeteria, here I come.

I FELT eyes on me as I made my way to the cafeteria, but ignored them. Auden had warned me he'd have to force some poor sap to follow me around, so I assumed the eyes belonged to said poor sap.

Once again, the cafeteria quieted as I entered.

The line of fae scattered, leaving me with a clear path to the food.

Score.

A few of the servers murmured, "Queen Noa," and bowed their heads a bit as I passed them.

I ignored them. I was a normal girl; being called "Queen" weirded me out, for sure. And I still didn't understand the dynamic between the fae leaders and the rest of the fae, so all I knew was that Auden had told me they either wanted to *bed* me or kill me.

Which didn't exactly sit well with me, but the food was worth the risk. Auden seemed like just as much a danger as the rest of those guys, even if he'd protected me from Green-Haired Joge.

And speak of the devil...

As I made it out of the food line, I noticed that Green-Haired Joge sat at a table off to the side, full of fae.

And he was glaring at me; cool.

I saw an empty seat at the same table I'd sat on yesterday. In fact, it was the same empty seat I'd occupied the day before. New fae took the other seats, though; maybe they wanted to talk to me.

Sitting down in the empty seat, I picked up my fork and waited for the fae to scatter.

They didn't.

Instead, they stared.

I realized most of their plates were empty or nearly-empty; they'd been there for a while.

Waiting for me?

I didn't know. Wasn't sure I wanted to know, though.

"Queen Noa." One of them bobbed his head toward me.

I gave him a quick salute, my mouth already full of food.

"You're beautiful," one of the men blurted, then stared down at the table intensely.

Crap.

At least I had taken the time to put a shirt on. That was a good call.

I swallowed the food in my mouth. "Thanks."

"In the past, faery queens would take lovers," another of the guys said casually. He had pink hair; of course he was the horny dude talking about married people taking lovers.

I coughed. "Is that so?"

"Not all, but some," another of the men corrected. "Fae like to fight; it gave the men something to fight about." His hair was a deep purple color that reminded me of my old bra. Truthfully, I wasn't a fan of the color, but he rocked it.

"What do you fight about when there's no women?" I tried to change the subject.

"Land. Leadership." The pink-haired fae shrugged casually. "But we'd much prefer to fight over women."

Great.

Really, freakin' great.

"I'd like to warm your bed," the pink-haired one continued.

Uh-oh.

Holy shit.

I was legitimately being propositioned. By someone who knew I was married.

What the hell was wrong with this guy?

Pink-Hair continued, "Considering the king is young and inexperienced, I doubt he knows how to pleasure you. Plus, he's a boring wist. I can make you feel far better."

There was that fae curse I didn't understand.

And... a lot of other crap.

"You said there aren't any women in Avalon," I pointed out.

The man stared at me, waiting for me to get to my point.

In fact, all of them were staring at me.

"So, aren't you all inexperienced when it comes to... bed-sharing?" I gestured to the whole group of them.

I wasn't exactly shy when it came to my body or to sex; I'd done the obligatory one-night stands that left me feeling like shit once or twice a year ever since I lost my virginity to my high school boyfriend. But clearly, these men were assholes, or clueless, or clueless assholes.

"We're quick learners," the purple-haired fae countered.

"You've never had sex, so you have no way of knowing that," I pointed out. "And from where I'm sitting, it doesn't really seem like you've got much to offer me. Come on; I'm the queen." It felt insane to say that, but I definitely wasn't leaving these assholes to think there was a chance I'd sleep with them.

"A queen without a king who can please her."

My eyes narrowed, and I leaned over the table, toward them. They were only hitting on me because I was the only available vagina; I knew that without a doubt, and it made me the opposite of horny.

"Who says Auden hasn't learned to please me?"

There was a beat of silence, and tension rose.

Forcing my body position to remain as casual as possible, I leaned back. "The king is very passionate; I can assure you of that. I have no need of another man."

The fae's eyes grew a bit rounder.

I took another bite of my potatoes. If they pushed again, I'd go off on them about how much I despised cheaters.

My biological mom had cheated on her fiancé—my grandparents' son—resulting in an unwanted pregnancy. Her baby-daddy hadn't wanted me, and she hadn't wanted me, and her fiancé hadn't wanted me... which led to me being raised by my bio-mom's ex-fiance's parents. They'd adopted me shortly after I was born, and I loved them to death even if they weren't technically my blood-related grandparents.

My complicated origin story had been really hard to deal with when I was a young teenager, and I had become one of the most anti-cheating teens that ever existed. Since then, I'd helped a couple of the waitresses I worked with get revenge on their cheating exes.

Anyway, there weren't many things I despised the way I despised cheaters. And I sure as hell would never be one. If the sacrificial marriage I'd entered into never became a happy one, I'd be content with living alone in some kind of fae cottage with a bunch of pet cats or squirrels or whatever animals existed in Avalon, and a piano.

Hell, even just a pet *piano* would be fine. The piano was the only non-negotiable part of that potential future.

"So you won't be taking any of us up on our offers?" Pink-Hair gestured to the five fae at the table.

"Nope. I have no need for another lover." I continued eating.

Three of the fae got up—including the pink-haired and purple-haired ones. If they thought propositioning a woman was all it took, they were in for a rude awakening. Most of us liked at least a little conversation to go with our *bed-sharing*.

The one who'd blushed earlier stayed; he had orange hair and light skin. The only other one had remained quiet while I talked, and he had light green hair and dark skin.

"What are your names?" I asked them, so I could stop identifying them by their outlandish hair colors.

"I'm Ered," the green-haired one said.

"Voll," the blushing one mumbled.

"I'm Noa." I held out my hand.

Both stared at it, like it was a snake or something.

"Humans shake hands when they meet new people sometimes. It's getting a little outdated, I guess, but my grandpa always liked to say that he knew whether or not he'd like a person as soon as he shook their hand," I offered.

Both fae looked at me like *I* was the alien instead of them, but Ered finally took my hand and shook it awkwardly.

He lifted his eyebrows in surprise. "Your skin is very soft."

I huffed out a bit of a laugh. "Thanks, I guess."

The man released my hand, taking my wrist and frowning down at the skin.

"Okay, that's enough. Women don't like being touched without permission." I withdrew my hand, and his expression grew a bit grave.

"I'm sorry. I wasn't aware."

"It's fine. You've got to learn somehow." I offered my hand to Voll, and he tentatively took it. He was overly gentle, barely moving it at all.

"Wow. It is really soft." He looked at Ered with surprise in his eyes, and Ered nodded.

I took my hand back. "Humans don't keep ourselves busy by fighting like you do. I serve food, and play the piano."

They looked confused by that last bit.

CHAPTER 8

I SPENT the rest of my lunchtime explaining what a piano was and the basic way it worked. They seemed fascinated, and I kept hoping one of them would volunteer to bring me a piano, but they didn't, and eventually, I headed back to Auden's place.

The king was still missing when I walked back through the doors. Not knowing what else to do, I grabbed some clean clothes and headed into the bathroom. I hadn't brought much as far as clothing went, so I was going to need a washing machine soon—and a few more pairs of clothing. But I was feeling better after all the piano talk with Voll and Ered. I guess some of the fae weren't so bad after all.

I dried off, wringing my buttload of hair out in the towel before stepping out of the shower. Pulling clothes on took all of one minute, and then I wrapped said buttload of hair in the towel so it wouldn't drip everywhere.

All that new hair was annoying me already.

I stepped out of the bathroom... and nearly had a heart-attack when I found a gigantic, angry blond fae sitting on the couch.

"Hey there," I said, awkwardly scratching the back of my neck. "Why are you angry this time?"

His face was a deep, dark red. I'd seen him angry, but never red before. To be honest, I kind of liked the flustered look on him.

"I've been congratulated by a handful of my men for learning how to pleasure my wife so thoroughly that she turned down the most attractive of my people."

I waited a beat, hoping there was more of an explanation coming.

It didn't come.

"Mmkay, well, given your current volatility level, everything you just described could make you angry in a number of different ways. So how about you just tell me what you're pissed about, and we can argue about that until you storm out of here."

My head jerked to the side as the ocean crashed precariously close to the house.

He was even angrier than I expected, apparently.

"You've been telling my men that we've been intimate." He glowered at me.

"The alternative was them assuming I'm on the prowl for lovers."

The ocean crashed near the house again.

"They propositioned you?"

"Yup. And before you ask, yes, I left the house. I'm a

human sacrifice—not a prisoner. Apparently, past faeries didn't care about being loyal to their obnoxious husbands with anger-issues, so your people assumed I was looking for someone to share my bed. If I told them I wasn't into casual hookups, they would've kept nagging. Because I told them we're sleeping together, they'll leave me alone."

Another wave crashed nearby—and this time, water slid into the house.

We both watched it flow in, slowing near our feet, and then flow out.

"Bed-sharing was far more than a casual hookup. It was a faery's way of declaring to the world that she regretted marrying her husband by letting other men take his place in her bed," he said, through gritted teeth. "It was very public, and the worst insult a wife could give her husband."

"In what world would a man willingly let another dude take his place in his wife's bed in the house he shared with her?" I countered.

"You ask too many questions without giving enough answers," he growled.

I rolled my eyes. "I was conceived by a woman cheating on her fiancé, and it messed with me as a kid. Now there's nothing I hate more than a cheater."

His eyes flashed with what looked like—but couldn't have been—interest for a moment before growing angry again.

"When a fae married a faery, everything he owned became hers. It's why we're not interested in large houses."

He gestured to the house. "Instinct tells us it won't be ours for long."

I lifted my eyebrows. "So this place is mine?" I gestured to the house, like he had.

"Unfortunately."

My eyes skimmed the space.

Not too shabby.

"So a woman could invite any man into her bed that she wanted, because it was *hers*, not *theirs*."

His head jerked in a nod.

The faeries of old sounded a heck of a lot more risqué than me. All I wanted to do was play my piano and eat good food.

"Well, I won't be inviting anyone into either of my beds, including you. So no need to get pissy." I peeled wet hair off the back of my neck and tried to dry it with the t-shirt I had on. "But if I were you, I'd just accept the compliment when they congratulate you for sharing my bed. They all think you're the man, now, and you didn't even have to do anything but yell at me."

His face reddened again.

"Look, I can see you're getting mad again, so I'm just going to quit when I'm ahead. If you cool off and want to have a real conversation about it—without any lecturing or shouting involved—let me know."

I walked to my room.

He caught the door as I reached for the knob, and I turned around with a silent sigh.

"Fae can't lie," he said.

I blinked up at him.

His eyes had creeped me out at first, but I was starting to think they were kind of beautiful.

"What?"

"Fae—and faeries—can't lie. The magic within us prevents it. If you were able to lie to the men at lunch, you haven't finished transitioning into one of us. When you're done, if you open your mouth to lie, you'll find yourself choking on the words."

Wow.

"Well, that sucks."

"And now that I've told you that, you owe me something."

I lifted an eyebrow. "I don't remember striking a bargain."

"You didn't." His eyes flashed in warning. "But if you want me to continue sharing information, you will too."

"Fine. I felt eyes on me today when I was walking to the cafeteria. If that wasn't because of you, and you're still planning to ask someone to follow me around, you should ask Voll or Ered to do it."

His forehead knitted together. "The soap-makers?"

Occupation hadn't come up during the conversation, so I shrugged. "I only know their names. But they're cool, and they didn't try to hit on me." I waited for him to demand more information, but he didn't. "Now, unless you're offering to carry me back to the other fae kingdoms so I can hang out with Hannah and Elyn, I'm going to take a nap." I gestured over my shoulder.

He said nothing but released the doorknob, and I stepped inside my room.

Making it to my bed, I climbed in and stared up at the ceiling.

I wasn't tired, though. I'd swam way more in the past day than I had in my entire life leading up to it, yet I felt less tired than I had in years.

Was the water somehow invigorating me?

I needed to ask my freakin' husband, but that would require talking to him.

Which would require offering more information about my own life, apparently. Which was ridiculous.

I heard the door open and close. Guess Auden was leaving, and taking my chance at learning about being a sea fae with him. I'd have to ask him next time I saw him... or find someone else who could answer my questions.

I'd prefer to find Voll or Ered, but they'd left the cafeteria when I had. And walking around while asking for directions just seemed way too typical *average human woman* not to get me killed.

But maybe the other fae kings would know.

And maybe they'd be more willing to tell me.

I sat up.

Looked like it was time to swim back to the earth castle.

"It would be nice to have a swimsuit," I mumbled to myself, stepping out of my room.

My eyes landed on the bag I'd seen next to Auden on the couch. My eyes had slid right over it, as if it wasn't there at all, focusing on the sexy, pissed-off fae. But if he'd left the bag there...

I grabbed it, and pulled a few gallon-sized freezer bags out of a waterproof fabric bag.

Were those *swimsuits*?

I unzipped the first bag, and pulled out three bikinis. They were all different designs and cuts, and I checked the tags...

The right size.

"You're good," I told Auden, though clearly he wasn't there.

I opened the next Ziploc bag, and found two one-piece swimsuits and a tankini.

The other two bags held different styles of swimsuit coverups, and at the bottom of one of the bags, was a handful of hair-ties.

"Wow. Thoughtful, and considerate. The colors are even good." He hadn't gotten anything brightly-colored or patterned crazily; I never wore things like that, unless you counted my purple bargain-bra, so it was a good call.

And, like I'd said, really thoughtful.

"Guess you're not just a big ole' grumpy jerk after all," I muttered, grabbing my favorite of the bikinis and heading back to the bathroom.

After I changed, I put the rest of the clothes on top of my suitcase, grabbed a thin coverup dress, and headed out. Swimming in a coverup might be annoying, but it was better than the alternative.

I headed out of the house, not feeling any eyes on me that

time. Whether Auden had called off his guard, or the "guard" had been some creep, I didn't know. But it was nice not to feel like I was being followed.

I slipped into the water, and my shoulders relaxed almost instantly. It felt insanely good, and I had to assume that was because of the magic now running through my veins.

Angling myself toward the place the dock had sat before Auden destroyed it (accidentally?), I waded out deeper.

As I began to swim, the steady movements were surprisingly relaxing. The ocean seemed to be welcoming me, wrapping around me, making me feel safe. I'd been terrified of sharks when I swam in the ocean during my senior trip with my grandpa, but the fear seemed to have disappeared. Whether that was because the water felt so comforting or because I'd grown up a bit, I didn't know.

When I reached the shore, I was actually a bit bummed that I was done swimming. My eyes skimmed over the water as I slipped out of my swimsuit coverup, wringing water out of it so it would dry a little faster. Not much came out, but I figured it was worth the effort anyway.

Since I didn't see any fae nearby, I headed toward the wooden gazebo. I was confident I could find the path that would lead me back to the stuffy, smelly earth castle.

As soon as I started down the dirt trail, I felt eyes on me again.

Maybe I hadn't thought my little escapade through all the way.

Maybe I should've asked for a guard... even if he was a

soap-maker. At least the soap-maker would smell good while making an attempt to scare off other fae.

"Whoever you are, don't even think about coming after me," I yelled into the trees around me. "My husband is the sea king, and he's an angry... wist. He'll screw you up badly if you try anything."

Okay, now I felt stupid for yelling at the trees and using a fae swear word I didn't know the meaning of. But maybe it would scare them off, and work to my advantage anyway.

"You're pretty," a male voice said from behind me.

I yelled and jumped, spinning around.

A gigantic fae—okay, they were all gigantic—with tan skin and pale pink hair walked a circle around me. I stayed still, hoping he was like a bear.

I was supposed to pretend not to be afraid, right?

Or was I supposed to run when confronted by a bear?

Crap, I couldn't remember.

"Chaos is lucky," the fae finally remarked. "It's too bad I'm not a king."

My hand planted on my chest, my breathing rapid. "Don't just jump out at people. Who the hell are you?"

"Octo." He held out a hand.

Why not?

I shook it.

"Soft skin," he remarked.

"I'm going to the castle," I gestured in the direction of the earth castle. "Looking for Hannah. I'm pretty sure Kalus is the earth king, not the sky king, right? She's with Kalus."

"Yup. King Kalus and his new wife are eating chocolatey

fruit in her castle right now." He bobbed his head. "I'll take you to them."

Well, that was surprisingly helpful. I guess I had learned that not all fae were absolute bastards, though. And he'd called the castle hers—which was a good sign that Auden was probably telling the truth about the whole women-own-stuff thing. "Thanks."

We started through the forest again, and he asked, "How's the sea castle?"

"They have really good food."

What else was I supposed to say? Auden accidentally flooded it because he was so pissed at me, and I've officially had three men offer to be my mistresses already?

Yeah, no.

I'd stick with the food thing.

He nodded. "The sea fae are known for their food."

Hmm. Good to know, I guess.

He didn't say anything else, and it occurred to me that Auden might've told me why.

"Are you waiting for me to share something? Since you just shared something?" I checked.

He glanced at me, his eyebrows furrowing. "Yes. The sharing of knowledge and thoughts should be equal."

Wow.

Okay, then. Useless information, useless information, useless information...

CHAPTER 9

OOH, I knew what to say.

"My favorite bar offers free peanuts," I remarked. "Most people don't eat them, though."

He looked surprised by that fact. "Interesting."

"Mmhm."

"Do you take the peanuts?"

"I don't know. What else are sea fae known for?"

His lips curved upward as he realized I was playing on the same knowledge-swap thing.

"Their tempers, and their constantly-changing royalty."

Weird.

Not the temper thing, but the changing-royalty thing.

"I don't eat the peanuts either. If I'm hungry at the bar, I usually order chili fries."

"What are chili fries?"

I shot him a look, and he flashed me a grin. "Chaos took over as king only a few hours before we were kicked out of

Avalon. Some other fae had been trying to talk him into taking over for years, but he refused until the previous king voted to get us sent to earth."

Geez.

"Chili fries are French fries—basically just potatoes, cut up and fried or baked—with all kinds of delicious goodness piled on top. Chili's usually beans and meat and cheese, and some other stuff," I explained, as we approached the castle.

"It doesn't sound good," the fae remarked.

"It tastes incredible, though."

The fae stopped at the doors, and nodded at me. "I'll wait here to walk you back to the ocean."

"That would be great, thanks." Surprisingly enough, I meant it. "Auden will probably come looking for me, all ragey, by then though. If he shows up, don't worry about it."

He bobbed his head again. "Have fun." Slipping back into the forest, he disappeared into the trees.

With a shake of my head, I stepped into the castle.

Music, playing in another room, had me speed-walking through the dirt-colored hallways. The music wasn't coming from a piano, but I was desperate for any music after the last forty-eight hours of assuming I'd never touch a piano again.

I stopped in the doorway when I saw Hannah sitting on a couch beside Kalus, dipping strawberries in a chocolate fountain.

My mouth watered immediately.

Kalus turned around, and his face split in a grin. "Noa!"

Hannah jumped up, her face lighting up as she crossed the room to throw her arms around me.

She even freakin' smelled good. How was this her arranged marriage, when mine consisted of a flooding house and me getting glared at for hunting down a cafeteria?

"Are you guys seriously in here eating chocolate fondue without inviting anyone else? Is this, like, a *date*?" The last word came out more judgy than I intended. If Hannah wanted to date or sleep with her sexy fae hubby, that was totally up to her. I just wanted to punch mine in the face and move on.

Hannah gave me a sheepish smile. "It's not a date. I told him I was craving chocolate, and he set this up."

I glanced over at the setup. A massive table of various foods to dip in a chocolate fountain, a few fae playing violins, and—

"Is that a piano?" My eyes jerked back to Hannah.

Of course it was a piano. I had eyes. But asking seemed more socially-acceptable.

Her head bobbed. "None of the fae here know how to play it."

Screw the chocolate—I was spending time with the piano.

"Go back to your date," I called out, speed-walking over the piano.

I wanted to hug it. Would that be weird?

I decided it would be, but did it anyway.

It was just a little upright piano, even smaller than the one I had back home, but it could've been an electric keyboard and I would've been equally thrilled.

Hannah came over and leaned up against the wall as I

wiped my hands on my now-dry swimsuit coverup in an attempt to clean them. They weren't dirty; it was just a habit.

And luckily, I seemed to dry off much faster now than I used to.

My fingers launched into a few warm-up chords, and my eyes closed as something within me seemed to steady. The music felt *right* in a way nothing else had ever been able to compare to.

Except maybe the ocean, now, but that was a new development.

My hands launched into one of my favorite songs: *Hallelujah* by Leonard Cohen. I had many of my favorites memorized by heart, because there was something magical about being able to play with my eyes closed and just feel the magic of the music channeling through my soul and fingers.

I wasn't a romantic when it came to love, but when it came to music... well, that was a different story.

The song slowed and quieted as it approached the ending.

"Wow, Noa," Hannah stared at me. "You're incredible."

I hated getting compliments on my playing; what was I supposed to say?

Thanks, I think so too?

Oh, I don't play to be good?

Please don't talk about it?

I'd rather people just listen and then pretend they hadn't heard it at all, as ridiculous as that sounded.

"Thank you," I murmured, launching right into another

song. In a few minutes, I'd stop and try to question the earth king—but first, I needed to play for a bit.

Hannah went back to her chocolate fountain, and I eyed it as my fingers flew across the keys. It did look good...

My gaze dropped back to the keys, and I forgot about the chocolate.

At least twenty minutes must've passed by the time I reluctantly stopped playing and slipped off the bench, heading over to join Hannah and Kalus on the couch. They weren't sitting all snuggled up together or anything—so I'd probably been wrong about the date thing. Hannah didn't really seem like the type to jump in bed with a fae king, anyway.

Though who would've blamed her if she had?

He was freakin' gorgeous.

It was time to get my head back in the game, though.

"So, what can you tell me about the sea fae?" I asked Kalus, settling down beside Hannah. She handed me a strawberry drenched in chocolate, and I didn't waste a second before shoving that sucker in my mouth.

"Depends what you can tell me in exchange," the earth king said, his eyes mischievous.

Hannah rolled her eyes toward me. "This is how he answers every question. He now knows nearly everything about my childhood, yet I've only gotten like six facts out of him because I keep forgetting to demand his information."

I flashed her a grin. "Get your head in the game."

She grinned back. "I really need to."

We both looked at Kalus.

"I think my brother's looking for me," he drawled, getting up and strolling out of the room like he didn't have a care in the world.

"That's what happens whenever I do remember to ask." She threw her hand out toward him. "He wants me to just sit around batting my eyelashes and eating chocolate. And I'll take the chocolate, but I'm not a doll."

"I get that. At least Auden's sincere, I guess. Even if he's sincerely an asshole."

Her forehead wrinkled. "Has he tried to hurt you? I know we can't do much, but if we team up, we might be able to figure out a way to stop him somehow."

I waved off her worries. "No, he hasn't hurt me. He actually protected me from someone else, and bought stuff for me. I think the asshole-ness is just a front, but it's a really good front. Who knows how long it'll take me to break him down," I grumbled.

She relaxed a bit. "That's good; I've been worried about you. Kalus kept telling me that I didn't need to worry and that Auden was a good guy, but he lies."

"Actually, fae can't lie," I said.

Her eyebrows shot upward. "What?"

"Auden hasn't told me much, but he told me that. I sort of lied to a few of the other guys about sleeping with Auden so they'd stop hitting on me," I admitted sheepishly.

"You WHAT?"

I launched into the story, and she ended up laughing so hard she was crying.

"So what else did he tell you about the fae?" She asked.

Hannah seemed as hungry for information as I was. I wished I knew a way to get to Elyn too, so we could include her in the conversations, but I was pretty sure the sky castle was on top of that gigantic mountain, and there wasn't a chance in hell that I'd try to scale that thing.

Not even maybe.

"When a fae man marries a woman, she officially owns all of his stuff," I offered. "And when a fae tries to lie, they get all choked up and can't talk. Since I was able to lie today, Auden doesn't think we're fully-transitioned to being faeries."

Hannah nodded slowly, her forehead knitted together. "Kalus told me everything he has is mine, but I thought that was just a figure of speech. He sounded like he was joking."

"He might've been joking, but it was the truth. I guess some of the faeries would invite other guys into their beds to spite their husbands, since the faeries themselves owned the beds. It sounds like they've got a pretty screwed-up society to me."

Hannah made a face. "No kidding. Kalus told me that the fae are constantly fighting. As soon as one war ends, the next begins, because they're so bored and angry."

That didn't sound far-off from what I'd heard.

WE SPENT HALF an hour discussing what we'd learned about the fae—not incredibly much—before Auden stormed in.

"That's my cue." I winked at Hannah, and she grinned

back. "Hey honey, how was work?" I called out to my *husband*, making my voice sound as innocent as possible.

His forehead wrinkled, his gaze sliding up and down my figure before he scowled again. "We're leaving."

Turning, he left the castle.

"Of course we are." I followed him out a bit before stopping and calling out to Hannah, "Let's do this again soon. If you see Elyn, tell her to come too."

"Will do," she called back. "Be safe!"

The words suddenly reminded me of my grandpa, and the memory and longing hit me so hard it legitimately took my breath away.

The doors to the room she was in closed behind me as I took a few steps forward before I stopped and grabbed the wall, forcing myself to continue breathing.

"What?" Auden growled at me, stopping beside me.

"It's nothing. I'm fine," I wheezed, struggling for air.

The loss hurt something fierce.

I batted my eyes quickly, trying to blink the tears away before they could fall.

"Another lie?" Auden sounded pissed. "What the wist is wrong with you?"

"I still don't know what that word means," I said, brushing tears with the back of my hand.

Gentle palms landed on my shoulders, turning me away from the wall carefully.

"I told you not to touch me," I said, blinking away some more tears.

He glared back. "You're crying."

"Looks like it, doesn't it?" I pushed his hands off my shoulders and stepped past him, our chests brushing as I moved away.

"November." He stepped up beside me. "What's wrong?"

"It's really none of your business." My voice sounded hard, even in my ears.

It had been months since I'd cried for Grandpa—I'd finally started living normally again. But hearing Hannah say those words... it just triggered my memories.

Happy memories; really damned happy memories.

But sad ones, because the one person who had cared about me that way was gone.

He had loved me so much—and I had loved him so much. He was my support system, and now, without him, I was alone.

Being alone sucked.

"Noa..." his voice was strained as he walked beside me.

It didn't sound angry, though.

"I feel like my chest is going to wisting explode if you don't tell me why you're crying," he said.

"Why? We're not really together."

He didn't respond, but the frustration came off him in waves.

"It's just memories, okay? No need to *care*." We stepped out into the forest.

Auden's frustration turned to anger when I didn't explain further, and the ocean rose to meet us before we even made it to the beach.

The waves soothed my soul the way only music usually did, and by the time we got back to the sea castle, I was mostly at-ease again.

My grandpa was in a better place; with my grandma. Watching over me. I didn't know what all I believed, but I did believe that. And I refused to accept any other answer.

A man as good, and kind, and loving as that one didn't deserve anything less.

The sun was down when we walked into the beach house, so I shut myself in my room and went to bed.

Grief worked in mysterious ways, but for me, sleep helped.

CHAPTER 10

I FELT BETTER the next morning. Still a bit sad, but despite the last night's tears, I didn't have a headache.

An angry knock at my bedroom door dragged me out of bed.

Good old Auden. At least his anger seemed reliable.

"We have to do another power transfer," Auden growled "Get out here and eat."

"I'm getting dressed," I growled back.

"You have one minute."

My lips tilted upward a bit.

After talking to Hannah about Kalus and his charming avoidance, I was actually kind of glad Auden was a dick. At least he wasn't trying to trick me or anything. Maybe his anger was covering up a good guy beneath it, but that wasn't the same as pretending to be something he wasn't.

That was just... living.

Surviving.

Dealing with a shitty hand consisting of an arranged marriage along with giving his power to some average human girl he'd never met before, in a place that wasn't his home.

I didn't know for sure, but based on everything I'd gathered, I would've put money on the fae-caused unnatural natural disasters being an unfortunate accident. Auden wasn't the nicest fae I'd met... well, he wasn't even close to that. But he wasn't a bad guy, either.

The door opened as I finished buckling the back of my bikini top.

Auden's eyes dipped straight to my boobs—and for the first time since we'd met, he reminded me of a normal guy.

His eyes were back on mine quickly, showing no evidence of any amount of attraction to me. "Good, you're done crying. Let's go." He stepped out into the living room, leaving the door open.

I followed him out, but stopped when I saw a massively-full plate sitting on the couch.

"You're a freakin' lifesaver." I said, dropping onto the couch and grabbing the plate.

See—he was a good guy. Maybe he just didn't realize it.

That didn't mean I was going to fall into his arms or anything. Even a good guy could be an obnoxiously-angry jerk.

But I still couldn't wait to put that food in my mouth.

"You have five minutes," Auden warned, stalking out of the house.

"Thank you," I called after him, digging my fork into the pile of hashbrowns.

I ate like a pig until my own personal drill sergeant came striding back in through the door.

"I'm coming, I'm coming," I grumbled, hauling the plate to the fridge and setting it inside. There was a surprising amount of food in there—I guess he really had gone shopping, or sent someone for groceries somehow.

I made my way back to Auden, and he disappeared out the door before I reached him.

THE THIRD POWER exchange was as gross and bloody as the last two, and like the last two, ended with Auden dragging me back to his beach house before disappearing.

We fell into a pattern for the next week; power exchange, argument, lunch, more arguing, me swimming over to the earth castle, hanging with Hannah and her dog (the earth king sent someone to retrieve him for her) after Kalus made his escape, and playing the piano until Auden inevitably showed up to drag me back to the beach house yet again.

The rest of the fae seemed to stay away from us for the most part, including Octo.

Voll and Ered were around frequently, though, which led me to believe that Auden may have taken me up on my suggestion to make them my guards.

But things started to change on the day of the tenth power transfer.

· · ·

MY HAND PRESSED to Auden's bleeding wound, me reaching up to his shoulder at that point to keep the magical scars climbing his arm.

He staggered backward as the wound started to close up.

Not expecting it, I staggered with him—and we both went down hard.

I landed sprawled out over his chest, staring down at him in shock. "Did you just fall over?"

I didn't know much about gigantic guys with gigantic muscles, but I was fairly sure that falling over wasn't something they did often. I'd definitely never seen one of the fae trip before.

"No," he grunted.

I let go of his arm, washing my hands in the tide just past his bicep as the ocean rolled up to meet us. "It sure looks like you did."

He dropped me on my ass on the sand, rising quickly.

The blood drained from his face, and he staggered again.

And then sat down on the sand.

"Crap. Are you sick?"

He scowled at me. "No. My power's being drained by a vixen with more hair than muscle."

Okay, rude.

"It shouldn't hurt, though. Should it?" I looked over at Ien, whose always-cheerful head bobbed.

"The kings have been dealing with the discomfort and weakness of being drained of their magic since day one. It will only get worse until we're back in Avalon."

My head jerked back to Auden. He had never

mentioned any pain or discomfort before; why was he keeping it a secret? "I haven't even felt the magic, though," I said.

"With only a fraction of the kings' magic, all you'll feel is a connection with the ocean, the way most low-power-level fae do," Ien explained.

My lips formed an 'O'.

So that was why the ocean always made me feel better.

"How much of their magic do we have to take? Elyn asked.

"My vision didn't tell me that." Ien shrugged. "We've been trying to open a portal using you every day, but it hasn't worked yet."

Geez, why hadn't anyone told us that? "What? I didn't know that."

"You're not one of us." Auden's voice was sharp and angry.

"Bullshit. Look at me." I gestured to my ears, and my bush of hair. "I'm definitely not human anymore."

"You're low-level faeries," Ien agreed, interrupting me and Auden before we could start arguing again.

We were pretty freakin' good at the arguing thing.

"Lie," Auden cut in.

I shot him a glare.

He glared back. "Do it. If you can lie, there's still some part of you that's human."

"Fine," I tossed the word out. "You're the nicest person I've ever met."

The lie left my lips without a problem.

"We must be missing something," Auden growled, looking back at Ien. "They've got enough power."

"You had a lot more scars in my vision," Ien pointed out. "We're transferring the power as fast as we can, but I think we're just going to have to wait the ladies out." He glanced at me, then the other girls. "Sorry."

I didn't know what he was apologizing for. At that point, it wasn't like we could go back to our old lives when all this fae stuff was over. I couldn't imagine the massive physical and magical changes were reversible.

"At this point, I think it's fair for us to ask to be allowed to live together," Elyn spoke up.

Hannah and I hadn't seen her outside the power transfers; Merzo, her sky king, had all but taken her hostage.

It would be nice to live with the other ex-humans, but I didn't imagine that would make Auden any easier to deal with.

"We need you in the kings' homes so the kings don't feel pain as their magic pulls them back to you," Ien said, not unkindly.

"Our homes, you mean," I cut in. "And why has no one told us about the pain?"

Ien paused, glancing at Auden.

The sea king glared back, of course.

Were they doubting the "our homes" thing? In case they were, I added, "The kings' homes became ours when we married them."

"Yes, that's correct," Ien's cheerfulness had up and vanished. "But it's dangerous for a king to leave his kingdom. The elements will call him, and the people will revolt."

Based on the few things I knew about the sea fae, I actually believed that. Most of them didn't seem to respect Auden very much, and he did spend a lot of time in the ocean.

I didn't like the guy, but I also didn't want to cause him pain. He had done a few thoughtful things for me, and I could return the favor.

"I can't leave my beach house," I told Elyn. "The ocean makes me feel too good."

She grimaced. "I guess the sky makes me feel that way too."

"Teach her to fly," Auden growled at Merzo.

Merzo's expression remained stony.

I'd learned from Hannah that the sky king and earth king were blood-related brothers. Kalus was the rougher of the two, but also the friendlier one.

"You can do that?" Elyn demanded, glaring at Merzo.

"Yes." His expression remained neutral as his eyes met hers.

She looked around, and when her eyes landed on a rock, she stalked over and grabbed it. With an angry cry, she threw it at him.

My eyebrows shot upward as the rock collided with his chest, bouncing off to hit the ground.

I didn't know much about fae magic, but Auden could manipulate the ocean in pretty much every way. So I was pretty sure Merzo could do the same with the clouds or sky or something. Which meant he could've stopped the rock, somehow.

But he didn't.

"I'm not a damned prisoner!" Elyn yelled, searching violently for another rock. She grabbed it out of the dirt, and launched it at his head.

He took one step to the side, ensuring that the rock hit his shoulder instead of his head.

"I'll teach you how to fly," he grunted.

"You'd better!" She launched another rock.

It would've gone over his shoulder, but he stepped to the side and it collided with his neck.

Was he helping her hit him?

Yeah, I didn't understand fae dudes. At all.

"I'll teach you at home," Merzo told Elyn, as another rock hit him.

"No. I'm not going anywhere with you until you show me."

Merzo's lips formed a flat line, and he looked at the other two kings.

"That's our cue, love," Kalus slung an arm over Hannah's shoulder and towed her away from the beach, countering her protests with flowery compliments and obvious avoidance.

"Come on," Auden told me.

An obvious contrast to the earth king's sweet words, but I preferred the simple communication Auden and I had so clearly not perfected.

"Visit me," I told Elyn with a quick grin, before wading into the water after the sea king.

"I will." She flashed the sky king a glare that told me he was going to regret keeping it from her in the first place.

Auden dove into the waves, and I dove after him.

My body slipped through the water smoothly, in a way that it had never moved through the air. Something about it just felt *right*. Like I belonged there.

CHAPTER 11

AUDEN WAS ALREADY in our house when I got out of the
water and wrung my hair out.

Cupboards slammed as the fae king searched for
something.

I headed into the kitchen, leaning up against the fridge as
he grabbed a pan. "What are you doing?"

"I'm making you lunch," he snarled at me.

"Okay."

He paused, those strange eyes flashing at me. I was
starting to get used to their strangeness... and starting to
think they were kind of beautiful. "You're not going to
argue?"

"Not this time."

He seemed slightly less angry when he opened the fridge,
moving me with the door and then giving me a light push
back to the door after he closed it.

Eggs cracked quickly and violently into a large pan, and

then meat and cheese were dropped in with it, and Auden's gigantic hand was whipping a fork through the mixture.

I watched him work for a few minutes, and the tension in his shoulders seemed to ease. I'd noticed that he didn't like to sit around; he never seemed to stop and read a book, or take a nap, or just relax.

I wondered why, but knew he wouldn't respond well to me asking, so I kept my mouth shut about that.

"How weak are you compared to where you were?" I asked instead.

He whipped the eggs harder.

Weaker, I guess.

"Is my connection causing you pain?" I checked.

He whipped faster.

Those eggs were going to be fluff by the time I finished questioning him, at that pace.

I continued, "I turned Elyn down on the beach to make things easier for you; by your own logic, now you owe me something."

He shot me a narrow-eyed stare. "I'm making you food."

"If that's my payment for having your back, I'll walk to the cafeteria so I can get something else."

He growled, shoving a hand through the wild, silky-looking hair falling into his eyes. "You're so wisting stubborn."

I itched to ask what the curse meant, but knew that would consume whatever he felt like he owed me. And I wasn't cool with that.

"Right back at you."

He scoffed, focusing back on the eggs. "The first day, the bond between our magic gave me about a mile of leeway. It's progressively gotten worse. Now, just a room or two is painful. Soon, I'll be glued to your side just to avoid the feeling that I've been ripped in two."

I blinked.

Feeling like he was being ripped in two couldn't have been pleasant, but considering a near-future where we couldn't be more than a few feet apart was... a lot.

I'd probably lose my mind, spending that much time with the man.

"Why do you spend so much time in the water?" I asked, hoping his generosity would keep him answering my questions while his over-whipped-omelet cooked.

He shot me a glare, instead.

A sigh escaped me. "I play the piano in my free-time."

"I already know that. I've heard you play."

Right. He'd interrupted me a number of times to drag me back to the beach house.

I hadn't considered that my escapades to the earth castle might be causing him physical pain, though. And I felt unexpectedly-shitty for doing that to him.

"I used to take existing songs and change them up a bit, changing the beat and the emotion behind them. Before you guys came and... broke the world. I recorded videos, and put them on the internet. Never made more than a couple hundred bucks a month from it, but it was worth it to me."

He removed the omelet from the pan, and put the plate in my hands before giving me the answer I was looking for. "Your planet's oceans respond to my emotions, for whatever reason. Being in the water makes it easier to remain calm enough to keep the waves from raging with me."

He handed me a fork and turned off the stove.

"Does the ocean make you feel calm, like it does for me?" I asked him, striding over to the couch.

He didn't answer me, instead walking out of the house and out to the water again.

I rolled my eyes. If he wanted to cause himself pain by being away from me, that was his call—I was going to eat my food.

WHEN I WAS DONE EATING, guilt tugged at my conscience. I couldn't see Auden, but figured he hadn't gone far. It had sounded like the connection between us hurt more the further he went from me.

I hoped moving a bit closer to him would ease any pain he may be feeling, so I headed outside. My toes sank into the sand as I walked, and the ocean swept up the beach to meet my ankles.

I dropped to my ass on the damp sand, watching the waves sweep up toward me. The water washed over my feet, sliding up my calves and stopping at my knees before sliding back to join the rest of the ocean.

I didn't know how close Auden was, but I assumed he'd found a comfortable resting place at the bottom of the ocean or something. He could breathe underwater, like I apparently could, but I'd never tried it since I still didn't want to drown.

Movement in the sky a ways above me caught my eye. My lips curved upward when I saw Elyn and Merzo in the air.

They flew over to me, and descended until their bare feet met the sandy beach.

I grinned at her. "You made it."

"Yes! Flying is easy!" she exclaimed, then shot Merzo a glare.

His eyes flicked to her, and then he took off from the ground. Heading back up toward his castle, I assumed. Though it was far enough away that maybe he wouldn't go all the way—maybe he'd just hang out in the sky or something so he didn't end up in pain.

The clouds swallowed him, and Elyn collapsed to the sand beside me. "I owe your king a thank-you. That was really cool of him to tell Merzo to teach me to fly."

A little annoyance tugged at me.

He had never taught me anything like that, yet he'd stood up for Elyn.

Did he wish he'd picked her before Merzo could?

Probably. I was the last choice, after all.

Why did that irritate me so much? I needed to get over it.

"Yeah," I nodded.

It had been cool of him to tell her; that was undeniable.

"What have you been up to in your sky castle?" I asked, gesturing up into the sky.

"Reading, mostly." A yawn stretched her lips. "Merzo

pretty much ignores me. I've tried teasing him and arguing with him, but he's the equivalent of a brick wall."

I snorted. "You got the brick wall, and I got the angry hurricane."

She grimaced. "Surprisingly enough, I think I'd choose the hurricane."

I ignored more of that annoying irritation when it rose up again.

No way was I letting that fester.

"Did Merzo teach you anything else?" I asked Elyn. "Hannah and I have been trying to learn all we can about the fae, but they're close-lipped about pretty much everything. We can't even get them to teach us about the magic we now have."

She shook her head. "He really just ignores me. When I ask questions, he either stares at me or walks away."

I grimaced. "That does sound annoying."

Auden did something similar—but only sometimes. I had still learned some things from him.

"What's the sky castle like?" I checked.

"It's beautiful," she admitted. "There are massive glass windows everywhere, so you can look out at the world for miles. And there are loads of comfortable couches, and shelves upon shelves of books. If I wasn't so lonely in there, I could stay forever."

"Sounds awesome. If you can fly with a passenger, you should drag Hannah up there. She's huge into reading, but Kalus doesn't have many books."

Elyn's eyes brightened. "I'll try that."

I was glad I wasn't going to be the one she tried flying with. I'd probably survive a fall into the water, given my body's newfound love for the stuff, but I didn't want to test that with someone who'd just learned to fly.

"So where's your hurricane?" she asked, glancing over her shoulder at the beach house.

"Out there somewhere." I gestured toward the ocean. "Probably not too far. Apparently the pull of the magic causes him pain when he's more than a room or two away."

Elyn's eyebrows shot upward. "Does it work like that for all three of them?"

I shrugged. "I want to say yes, but there are probably a few factors and I don't understand any of them well enough to say for sure."

She made a face. "I'll have to try to ask Merzo."

"Good luck." I flashed her a grin.

She groan-laughed, and then changed the subject. "So if he can breathe underwater, can you?"

"Not sure." I shrugged. "He says I can, but I've been too afraid I'll drown to try it.

She grimaced. "I get that. Flying was terrifying at first."

"I can imagine."

"Well, if you want, I can keep watch while you test it out," Elyn offered, tucking a strand of her ruby-colored hair behind her ear. She made a face, shoving it backward again. "This stuff is so damned annoying. There's a reason I never grew it out. I tried cutting it off with a kitchen knife the other day, but it just grew back."

I snorted. "You cut your hair with a kitchen knife?"

A guilty grin tugged her lips upward. "Desperate times call for desperate measures."

"Apparently." I looked out at the ocean with a sigh. "Alright. I'm going to do it."

"You've got this." Elyn held her hand out for a high-five, and I slapped my palm to hers.

It was weird; the support system the three of us had sort of started becoming. Nice, but weird.

I stood up, heading out deeper into the water. It seemed to rise to meet me, but that had to be my imagination.

"If I don't come up in a minute, drag my drowning ass out of the water," I called to Elyn.

She gave me a thumbs-up, and I kept going until the water was around my chest.

Crouching down, I vowed to myself that I'd haunt Auden if I drowned because of what he'd told me.

Letting out a breath of air, I dipped my head underneath the water. My eyes were squeezed shut tightly as I opened my mouth. The water didn't taste salty to me anymore—another random thing I assumed the fae were to thank for.

When my lungs started to burn, I forced myself to take in a deep breath... of water.

It felt weird sliding down my throat, but then things got weirder. My stomach didn't rise as I inhaled... instead, the water rushed right out through slanted gills over my ribcage.

I gaped down at the slits in my skin. They looked natural, as if they'd been there forever, but they most certainly had not.

A flash of silverish-white caught my eye, and all of the air —water—left my body when I saw what was over my legs.

A tail. It was a freakin' *tail*.

I was a mermaid. A freakin' MERMAID.

Small hands grabbed me by the biceps and dragged me upward.

"Was that a fish?" Elyn's head jerked from side to side as her eyes scanned the water.

I knew what she was looking for though.

The slits on my ribcage closed up as my body reverted back to breathing air. My feet kicked—separately—automatically going back to their typical form.

"Holy shit, I'm a mermaid," I panted.

"What?" Elyn's eyebrows shot upward.

"When I breathed the water, it changed me." I gestured frantically to my legs. "I had gills. And a tail. I'm a freakin' mermaid!"

"What? How? Show me!" she demanded, dropping her hold on my arms. I splashed down into the water.

"Okay, just don't freak out."

She gave me a look that said she would most definitely freak out.

I didn't care, though.

Submerging my head again, I focused on taking a deep breath of water in... and just like that, the slits on my ribcage opened back up to let the water out.

I heard a shout above the water, and saw splashing as Elyn jumped or something. My shocked eyes met my tail, running up and down it. It was longer than I'd expected a mermaid tail to be, and a bit fatter, too. My skin seemed to have taken on an even paler, shimmering sheen, and contrasted the silvery white scales nicely.

But it was still really freakin' weird.

I popped my head out of the water.

"Did you know the fae were mermaids?" Elyn demanded.

I shook my head. "Not even a clue."

"Is it just the sea fae? Or do you think the other fae are mermaids too?"

I shrugged, still reeling from the mermaid thing too much to focus on thinking clearly.

"Or maybe they change in different ways." Elyn's eyes were bright and determined. "Do you know any talkative fae?"

Only the light-pink-haired one, but I hadn't managed to find him again since that first day. "That would be a negative."

"Damn." She frowned. "Hannah's king seems like the nicest of the three. Maybe we can get more information out of him."

"Maybe," I agreed.

I kind of wanted to try out my mermaid tail, though...

"Let's go talk to her, and try to corner him or something. You can swim, and I can fly?" she checked.

Well, that solved both of our problems. "Sure." I nodded.

"Alright." Mischief colored her eyes. "I'll meet you there."

She took off from the ground, and I dove back into the water.

CHAPTER 12

SWIMMING AS A MERMAID WAS A RUSH, and it was like nothing else I'd ever experienced before. The way the water carried me, worked with me, slipped over my skin... it was even more incredible than just normal swimming had become.

I did feel bad for moving further away from Auden, though.

But he could always track us down, if the pain got too bad. And then I could demand answers from him. I was really tired of all the secrets, so that didn't sound half-bad.

I expected it to feel good to change my tail back to my human legs, but surprisingly enough, it didn't. It didn't really feel like *anything*.

"Well?" Elyn asked.

"It was awesome," I admitted, with a grin. "I can't believe I'm saying this, but maybe I like being a faery."

"Wow. Okay, yeah, it's time to figure out how I can get a

tail," she declared. "There's got to be something good to go along with all this hair." She tossed a handful of bright red waves at me, and I grinned as it fell back around her face, even more wild than it had been.

We walked up the path, and Elyn stared up at the sky as we moved. "Maybe I can change into some kind of a bird or something," she remarked. "It felt good when I was flying—maybe it'll feel better when I've got feathers."

I snorted. "I thought you were hoping for a tail."

"I was, but it's probably more likely that I'm a bird."

"Have you seen any birds in the sky?" I checked. "You said you've got a lot of windows; maybe you would've noticed the other fae flying."

She frowned, considering it. "I don't remember seeing any birds. Ever."

Hmm. "Normal birds avoid threats, though, don't they? Maybe you're some kind of *big* bird, like a phoenix or a vulture or something."

Her nose wrinkled. "Since when are phoenixes and vultures on the same level? One's a mystical creature, the other is a bird of prey."

I shrugged. "Both can fly. Truthfully, I don't know much about flying animals."

I didn't know much about any animals, period. I'd tried to adopt a cat once when I was in second grade, but quickly discovered I was allergic to it. After we took it back to the shelter, we'd tried a dog—but I was allergic to them to. The whole thing had soured my sensitive little second-grade heart to having pets, and I'd never gotten back around to the idea.

Though, I babied my piano to the point where it could possibly be considered a pet in its own right.

But thinking about that only made me sadder that I'd had to leave it in my apartment.

We debated the possible pros and cons to being some kind of a bird-person as we made our way to the earth castle, and reached the building without a problem. I was somewhat confident my bond with Auden would drag him toward us, but out of the three kings, surprisingly enough he seemed to be the one giving us the largest amount of important information.

Walking in without knocking, I led Elyn to the room I usually found Hannah and Kalus in. It was empty, though, so I led her to the room I knew was Hannah's.

We knocked on the door, and waited.

She pulled it open a few minutes later, wrapped in a towel and with her hair dripping all over the floor. Her eyes lit up when she saw us. "Come in!" She opened the door wide, ushering us inside. "I always have to shower after the blood thing." Her shoulders shivered a bit. "I hate blood."

I nodded; we'd all seen her reaction to it every time we did a power transfer.

For me, Swimming back to the beach house usually made me feel clean enough not to bother showering right away, but then again, something about the salt water seemed to work well with my skin. Maybe that had to do with the mermaid thing.

"Noa's a mermaid," Elyn blurted.

Hannah blinked at us. "What?"

Elyn gestured toward me.

"Auden told me I could breathe water a few days ago. I tried it today… and it turned me into a mermaid. Gills, and tail, and all." I pointed to my legs, as if that would help explain it better somehow.

"WHAT?" she yelled.

Elyn and I both knew she wasn't really asking *what*. She was trying to come to terms with the insanity that our lives had become. And we understood that better than pretty much anyone else on Earth could.

"Can we change into mermaids too?" Hannah asked. "Can all fae change into mermaids?"

"Hannah, love?" Her bedroom door swung open, and Kalus filled the doorway. His eyes flicked between the two of us, a bit surprised, before lingering on Hannah. "Is everything okay?"

"Can I turn into a mermaid?" she demanded.

Understanding flickered to life in his eyes, and his gaze moved to me. "Noa dear, that wasn't your secret to tell."

"My wife's not your *dear*, Kalus," Auden growled in the hallway.

There he was; my knight in shining… scales.

Kalus shot the sea king a flippant smirk. "It's just a saying, Chaos. No need to get your panties in a twist."

The other ladies and I exchanged grimaces.

We'd seen from the beginning that Auden wasn't best buds with the redheaded king brothers, but we'd never seen them fight.

"Since you guys aren't giving us the whole story about

anything, we've got no choice but to share *everything* we learn," I told Kalus, since he'd seemed so annoyed that I'd shared a secret that 'wasn't mine'.

"Has it occurred to you that there's a reason we don't want you to know everything, Noa *dear*?" Kalus emphasized the *dear* just to piss off Auden, I was sure.

The blond king appeared in the doorway, shoving Kalus into the room.

"No fighting," Hannah said, stepping between both of the men. "What can I turn into, Kalus?"

His lips pressed together in a mocking smile and he said nothing.

"We're leaving," Auden told me from the doorway.

Shockingly, he looked just as pissed as always.

"I'm not going anywhere until they've got answers," I warned.

Auden muttered something under his breath—probably a stray "wist" since that word seemed to apply to every situation. "The sky fae have dragon wings, the earth fae are centaurs." He gestured to Elyn and Hannah, as he said it.

Both of their jaws dropped.

Kalus spun to face Auden, and I could practically feel the anger pouring off of him.

"Get behind me, November," Auden said through gritted teeth.

I didn't think that was the right time to argue with him, so I slipped away from the other women and stepped behind the sea king.

"They aren't sacrificial lambs," Auden growled at Kalus.

"They're faeries, now. Creatures of Avalon that deserve to live."

The words took a second to click for me.

Sacrificial lambs?

As in...

My stomach turned.

They were planning to kill us?

"That's why you won't tell me anything?" Hannah demanded, putting it together faster than I did "You're planning on *killing me*?"

"Ien saw it, and what Ien sees needs to happen," Kalus growled. "It's not our decision."

"Of course it's your decision!" she yelled back.

"We really are human sacrifices," Elyn breathed, her eyes wild.

"We're leaving," Auden told me.

"We're going with you," Hannah said, grabbing Elyn's arm and dragging her across the room. Kalus tried to grab Hannah, and Elyn slugged him in the face.

Her expression contorted as she shook out her fist, swearing at the pain while Hannah continued dragging her out the door, past us and into the hallway. Kalus held his nose—definitely broken, though given the speed that they healed, it wouldn't be for long.

Auden began, "I don't—"

I cut him off with an elbow to his muscular back and a glare at his shoulders, silently warning him not to prove me wrong about thinking he wasn't a terrible guy.

There was a long pause, and then Auden finally told the earth king, "All of the queens are under my protection now."

He turned, and his hand found my lower back as he propelled me down the earth castle's hallway. I ran into the other women, and ended up pushing all of them as Auden pushed me.

The earth started to quake beneath our feet.

"Is that him?" Hannah squeaked.

"Him or you," Auden growled. "Move faster."

All three of us started to jog. His freakin' long legs had no problem keeping up with us at a normal-for-him pace while we stumbled along the dirt path.

The earth began to quake harder.

"The plan was to kill us all along?" Elyn asked Auden.

Auden said nothing, but I was pretty sure that meant yes. Since he was a fairly new king, I imagined that the others didn't listen much to his opinions, because he didn't seem on board with the murder plan.

"I can fly us over the water," Elyn told Hannah.

She sounded a lot more confident about that than she had earlier.

Hannah agreed, and Elyn grabbed her by the arm. They shot up into the sky while Auden and I dove into the water. I inhaled water, and couldn't help the curve of my lips as my legs lengthened into a tail that flowed out behind me.

Auden swam beneath me, his silvery-white eyes raking over my streamlined body while mine took him in. His tail was proportional to the rest of his body, making him much bigger and longer than me. The gills on his abdomen were slanted at the same angle as the shimmery scars along his arms, and the silvery sheen to his skin made it difficult to take my eyes off of him.

I'd never imagined a merman would be attractive before, but damn.

Chapter 13

He torpedoed up toward the top of the water, and I followed. We surfaced together, and he didn't mention checking me out as he swam in and strode up the beach.

My eyes caught on his swimsuit, and I glanced down at myself. Not naked; phew. Apparently our clothes remained on us somehow?

"Why are we not naked?" I asked, gesturing to my covered chest as I caught up with him quickly.

"I've given you plenty of information today."

"Come on. I'll answer any question you want."

He shot me a look I couldn't read. "Your scales come up over your skin when your body shifts forms, so whatever you have on beneath them remains in place."

Crazy, but cool.

Elyn and Hannah landed just in front of the door to our beach house. "Merzo's coming," Elyn said, her eyes tracking the king as he streaked across the sky. Now that the secret was out, a pair of massive, glittering black wings were spread out behind him in the sky. "Any advice?" she looked at Auden, just in time to see him disappear into the house.

Hannah glared up at the sky. "He can't kill you until we get that portal up and running, so give him hell."

"Or play nice so the deadly fae king doesn't take you back to his lair?" I suggested.

He landed, and Hannah and I flanked Elyn.

"You bastard!" she swore, as she clenched her fists at her sides.

Guess she was going with Hannah's plan.

I kind of hoped she would swing at him, even though it probably wasn't in her best interest.

She yelled, "You've been planning on killing me this entire time! I'm not going anywhere with you; you can go back to your empty castle and rot for all I care. And I hope the bond between us makes you suffer, while you rot."

The way she stumbled over the words told me she wasn't very practiced at insulting people, but it was decent for a first try.

"I'm just trying to keep my home alive," Merzo said, his hands lifting in surrender. "There's no other way."

"Haven't you read any of the books in your massive library? There's always another way." She pointed up to the gigantic mountains in the distance, whose tops I couldn't see from the beach. "Get away from me."

"The power transfers have to continue," Merzo said, his voice low. "The only way we get back to Avalon is if there's a faery to open the portal herself."

A faery queen?

As in, one?

"I'll do it, then. Since Auden's slightly less murderous than the rest of you bastards," I blurted.

I'd probably regret that, but it was already out so it was too late.

Elyn didn't seem convinced. "You said it only takes one queen to open the portal? If that's true, then why did Ien take three?"

"Better odds," Merzo said, his voice flat.

"Give me a few weeks to figure out the power, and I'll get you back home," I said, forcing my voice to come out sounding a hell of a lot surer than I felt. "Leave Elyn and Hannah out of it."

Merzo studied me for a moment.

I knew what he was seeing; the last pick, the blond, the *average human.*

"Fine." He finally dipped his head in agreement. "One week. If you don't figure it out by the end of that time, I take my wife back."

His wings blew air everywhere as they carried him up into the sky.

"How close do you think he'll stay?" Hannah whispered.

Any distance between them would cause him pain, so I murmured, "Close."

We stood there for a moment as the wind blew and dark clouds gathered in the sky. I hadn't seen it storm since I'd been there, but I'd definitely witnessed the sky fae's magic in the days of rain and earthquakes after the fae had arrived. "Alright, let's go." I gestured them inside.

I'd never shared an apartment with another girl my age; the closest I'd ever gotten to sharing with anyone at all was with my high school boyfriend, a few months after we graduated. But that relationship had crumbled pretty fast in the weeks leading up to starting college, and we split up a few days before we were supposed to move across the country and into an apartment together.

He'd wanted the *college experience.*

I'd just wanted to make music.

I hadn't been serious with anyone since then, and I'd never had the desire to be.

Inside, I found Auden at the stove again, cooking aggressively. I hadn't known aggressive cooking was a thing, but he definitely made it one.

"We'll have to snuggle," I told the other girls, cringing inwardly as I pointed to my bedroom. There was only one bed.

Yeah, I'd really never been close with other girls.

"Better than snuggling a fae," Hannah called over her shoulder as she and Elyn headed into my room.

I hurried after them, picking up things I'd left on the floor and shoving everything back in my suitcase. "Sorry, it's a mess."

"It'll get messier when Hannah brings her dog," Elyn tossed out, collapsing on my bed.

Oof, yeah, I really wasn't looking forward to sharing.

But I wasn't going to throw them out on their butts as

sacrifices to the kings again, so sharing was the only real option.

Unless I wanted to ask Auden to share his bed.

But, no.

I'd just cuddle with the other women. It was fine; I'd survive.

"We'll have to go back for our stuff," Elyn told Hannah. "I can fly us there if you want?"

"That would be so much better than walking," Hannah agreed.

Both of them looked at me. "It's fine; go ahead." I waved my hand through the air. "You should probably try to beat the storm anyway."

I doubted they would; the clouds had looked pretty dark. But the storm probably wouldn't bother Elyn anyway, given that the ocean didn't really bother me. Maybe it would make her feel better, the way the water did for me.

The other girls headed out again, leaving me alone with Auden.

Now that my room was compromised, it didn't really feel like a sanctuary anymore, so I went ahead and walked out to the kitchen.

"Is that shrimp? Tell me you didn't catch it yourself." I leaned up against the fridge again, like I had the last time we were in the kitchen together.

He shot me a glare that didn't really answer my question.

"I'm sorry about inviting Hannah and Elyn," I said, tucking my hair behind my ear. "I didn't mean to go over your head. I just didn't see any other options. So... I didn't give you a choice in the matter, but thanks anyway."

He didn't respond, not that I really expected him to.

"So is this supposed to be shrimp scampi?" I checked.

No answer again.

"I actually love shrimp," I admitted, guilt weighing me down a bit. Since fae were all about bargaining information and emotions and shit, maybe offering some info free-of-charge would cure some of his resentment toward me. "Before my grandpa died, we would meet at this one steakhouse every Wednesday night, without fail."

I continued, memories coming back rapidly as I spoke. "He'd get this giant slab of steak with a double-serving of broccoli, as if that made it healthy. I'd get this plate of grilled shrimp, with a salad doused in ranch and bacon, and a cup of mashed potatoes that grandpa pretty much always ended up eating for me. I tried going back without him a few times, but ended up sobbing in my car in the parking lot. I still have dreams about the shrimp though, because that's how good they were."

Auden didn't respond, though the anger lines around his eyes did vanish.

"We don't have to be enemies, you know," I remarked. "You seem to have plenty of those. I might be average, and a faery, and a human sacrifice, but we can still be *acquaintances*. The world wouldn't end."

The anger lines were back around his eyes. "I'll let you know when dinner's ready." He stirred the pasta violently once again as he gave me a clear dismissal.

At least I'd tried.

With a silent sigh, I slipped out of the kitchen and into my bedroom.

The other girls got back with Hannah's dog and the clothes the fae had given her just in time to eat. Auden left after dishing up the pasta, not bothering to stay long enough to eat with us.

I didn't comment on his departure, and neither did the other women. We were alive, and that was what really mattered. And I didn't think Auden was planning on murdering me, so that was a plus.

Though to be honest, with a temper like his, who really knew what he was capable of?

As we sat down, I noticed that my bowl had a much heavier serving of shrimp than the other two ladies', and while it could've been purely accidental, Auden was the one who'd handed me the bowl. And I'd told him how much I liked shrimp.

So, I doubted it was a coincidence.

The girls and I stayed up pretty late talking about the lives we'd left behind, though they did more talking than me.

Hannah's dog, Angelo, was a massive yellow lab, and he immediately decided I was the perfect chair. She apologized for him assuming he was a little lapdog, and we all laughed it off, but I found myself enjoying the cuddly company surprisingly enough. And whether I'd just outgrown my allergies or my faery-ness had changed that part of me, I didn't get sniffly or rashy because of his presence, or the insane amount of fur he shed.

We squished into the bed after shutting off the lights late into the night, with Angelo between Hannah and me, and my body hugging the edge of the bed. I closed my eyes and tried to sleep, but the noise from all of my companions was too loud.

After tossing and turning enough to annoy even the happy dog snuggled up against my side, I grabbed some clothes and slipped out of the room, intending to take a shower.

The bedroom door closed quietly behind me, but when I turned around, I stopped.

Auden's gigantic body was draped over the couch, his eyes closed and his chest rising and falling. He seemed to be sleeping pretty deeply, with a blanket partially balled up on his stomach. His feet hung off the couch—one over the armrest, and one over the back.

Why was he sleeping on the couch?

He could've been guarding us, but that seemed unlikely since I was pretty sure he'd already assigned a few fae to follow me around like bumbling shadows.

Maybe he hated his bed?

Unlikely though; it looked just as comfortable as mine.

The only other possibility was that the bond caused him pain even across the house from me.

He'd said he was fine one to two rooms away from me, but his room was two away if you counted the living area... so maybe it was really more like one room.

Frowning, I turned away from the gorgeous sleeping man and stepped into the bathroom. It was about the same distance from the couch as my bedroom, so I figured he wouldn't feel my change in scenery.

I took a long shower, trying to relax my body, but my mind kept going back to Auden, sleeping on the couch.

And I felt bad.

CHAPTER 14

MY MIND CHURNED as I scrubbed myself with fae soap.

Ien said there would be many more scars before I could open a portal for them; would Auden and I get to the point where we couldn't even be more than a foot or two apart? Or would it get so bad that we needed to be touching?

I wasn't completely opposed to that; it wasn't like touching a sexy fae king would be the end of the world for me. But I'd rather we keep our hands to ourselves so I didn't end up feeling like there was more to our *marriage* than there really was. Auden clearly had some hang-ups about us even being acquaintances, which didn't exactly bode well for a future of anything resembling friendship.

All of that aside...

Sleeping arrangements.

The fae king didn't fit on the couch, and if I was draining his magic away, he probably needed his sleep. He'd sleep better in a bed, and I would too.

"Bunkbeds," I murmured to myself, making the decision on the spot.

If we were in a rom-com, the bed situation would've undoubtedly led to a night of accidental snuggling and maybe some "unintentional" hooking up, but I wasn't going near that possibility with a ten-foot pole.

Bunkbeds weren't classy, and they weren't all that attractive, and hell, maybe they wouldn't even be that comfortable. But they could probably keep Auden out of pain. And me, out of an accidental-cuddling-session in which I inevitably had an encounter with his morning-wood and ended up wondering if it was me or nature that had him so horny upon waking up.

The other option was just to slap another bed down in the room, but bunk beds were clearly superior because we wouldn't have to see each other while we were in them. And given our rocky non-acquaintance-ness, not seeing each other was clearly the better call.

I stepped out of the bathroom in my t-shirt and panties, having not bothered with anything else. Instead of relaxing me like I'd hoped, the shower had only keyed me up further as I prepared myself for the argument in which I tried to convince Auden that two grown-ass adults needed to sleep in bunkbeds.

My eyes landed on the now-empty couch, and I stopped in the doorway.

Auden stepped out of the kitchen, wearing that near-permanent scowl of his. "Can't you just pick one place and stay there?"

"That's what I wanted to talk about, actually." I didn't bother beating around the bush. All more conversation would do was give him more ammunition to use in his clear dislike for me. "I think we should get bunkbeds."

He blinked.

"They're when you stack two beds, one on top of the other, with stairs or a ladder leading up to the top. I know they're not ideal, but it would make it easier for you to sleep. And then I wouldn't have to share a bed with Hannah and Elyn and Angelo, so I would actually be able to sleep."

He blinked at me again.

"You'd have to share a room with me," I continued. "And we would still be un-acquaintances, which is what you want. We wouldn't have to talk or anything. It would just help with the connection thing." I gestured between us.

His expression remained neutral, and he didn't say anything for a moment.

I waited.

Suddenly, he strode out of the house.

I followed him, running into his back when he stopped only a foot or two in front of the door.

My gaze followed his line of sight, and I lifted my eyebrows when I saw a redhead sprawled across the sandy grass beside our house, snoring loudly.

"Kalus?" I asked.

The earth king's snore caught in his throat, and he sat up quickly as he looked around for threats.

What was the other king doing outside? Obviously, he

needed to be near the ladies who had taken my bed, but I hadn't expected him to sleep on the floor.

Guess he felt bad enough about planning Hannah's murder not to try to drag her back to his castle kicking and screaming.

"I need you to build me a bed," Auden growled at Kalus.

Kalus raised two sleepy eyebrows.

"Do it, and you can sleep on my couch for the night," Auden added.

Bargaining, I guess.

I doubted Hannah would be thrilled with Auden's deal, but if it got us our bunkbeds, she'd have to get over it.

The earth king paused, considering it, before finally nodding. "Fine."

Auden glanced up at the roof of the house. If I squinted, I could make out the shape of someone sitting up there. Auden called out, "Find me another mattress and you can have it tomorrow night."

The sky king flew up, off my roof.

"Why do they listen to you?" I asked Auden.

He didn't answer, because he was him.

To my surprise, Kalus did answer, though. "In Avalon, all three of our kingdoms are nearly equal sizes and numbers. We all possess an equal amount of the land. Here, the sea vastly outweighs and overpowers us. You may not believe it, but we do have a code."

"And the one with the most land is in charge?" I checked.

Sounded like a near-guarantee for corruption.

"Mmhmm. Why am I building a bed?" Kalus asked.

The give and take of fae conversation. Lovely.

"We need another bed." I shrugged; the answer seemed pretty obvious. "With Hannah and Elyn in here, it's full."

"Ah, but you're warming each other's beds," Kalus' expression grew cunning. "We've all heard how well Chaos here pleases you."

Crap.

Lie time.

Hopefully Auden's magic didn't try to choke me out for it.

"Having sex and actually sleeping together are vastly different. This is still an arranged marriage." I gestured between myself and Auden as we stepped inside the house.

"Hmm." Kalus didn't look quite convinced, but he did look a bit disappointed that I hadn't mumbled and bumbled about us not actually sleeping together.

Auden looked even more irritated with me than usual— not easy—as he and Kalus headed for his room while I took a quick detour into the other bedroom.

Hannah and Elyn were already stirring. "Hey," I whispered. "Your kings are in the house, helping us move stuff around. I'll keep them out of here."

Elyn murmured an agreement and fell back asleep, but Hannah's eyes remained cracked open. "Tell us when they leave?"

I nodded, and slipped out of the room.

"I think one's supposed to go over the other one," Kalus remarked.

Stopping in the doorway, I watched the floor morph as sleek, black stone grew upward, lifting the mattress with it.

"Move the top lower," I told him, stepping a bit into the room. "There has to be enough space at the top so the person up there doesn't smash their head into the ceiling."

Kalus conceded with a nod, and the rock-made bunkbed shrunk down a bit.

I bit back a snort at the irony of two all-powerful fae kings working together to build bunkbeds, of all things.

A shirtless Merzo stepped into the house, carrying a gigantic mattress awkwardly but not with difficulty. My eyes snapped to the scaly wings protruding from his back, and my lips rounded a bit as I saw where they seemed to slide back into his spine. The scales looked softer than silk, and the wings looked like they belonged there nestled into the ink on his shoulders.

No wonder he wasn't wearing a shirt.

Merzo dropped the mattress in the open space beneath the first.

"How's that?" Kalus looked at me.

"A little lower, still," I said.

The top mattress moved down a few more inches.

"Okay, stop. Now it just needs a railing around the top edge, and a ladder." I gestured to the side.

A stone ladder and simple railing grew out of the bunkbed frame, and then Kalus looked at me again.

"Perfect. Thanks." I nodded toward him. "Don't go near the other bedroom."

He scowled, but dipped his head before striding out of the room.

I glanced at Merzo. "You can sleep on the floor if you don't want to sleep on the roof." I could hear it raining outside; that wasn't exactly a pleasant sleeping arrangement.

But he was causing the storm, so maybe he didn't mind.

"I'll stick to the roof. The couch is mine tomorrow." He shot a narrow-eyed look at Auden.

The sea king scowled back. "I keep my word."

"Unlike your predecessors?" Merzo called over his shoulder as he strode out of the room.

I heard the ocean's tide change a bit outside. I was growing accustomed to its presence, getting used to the way it normally sounded, which made it easier to tell when Auden's magic was affecting it.

"The previous sea kings were bastards, I take it," I remarked.

"Go to bed," he told me, grabbing some clean sheets out of the closet and striding over to the bottom bunk. He had the sheet on in the blink of an eye, and was draped out over the mattress just as fast.

Guess I was taking the top.

I climbed the ladder. It was really sturdy—much sturdier than the ladder on the loft bed I'd has a kid. I had loved that bed, but settling onto the top bunk of the bunkbed, I wasn't sure why I'd liked the loft.

There was something really unappealing about staring up at the ceiling while it was so close, and it made my chest feel a bit tight.

But I'd be fine.

Rolling to my side, I buried myself under the blankets. They smelled of the ocean; the way it smelled to me now that I couldn't sense the salt like I'd used to.

I was nearly asleep when I remembered I needed to go check in with the other girls.

With a sigh, I climbed back down the ladder and crossed the house.

"Swear that you're not going to bug or hurt the other women in any way?" I asked Kalus as I passed. Since the fae couldn't lie, his promise would be binding.

"Yes," he grumbled, trying to get comfortable on the couch. It was much smaller than he was, but Auden had managed to find some semblance of comfort, so I imagined Kalus could too. They were about the same size, anyway.

"They're gone?" Hannah murmured when I stepped back in.

"Kalus is sleeping on the couch, Merzo's on the roof," I said, apologetically.

Hannah's eyes opened wider.

"They swore they wouldn't hurt either of you, and they can't lie," I reminded her. "And they were sleeping outside earlier, we just didn't realize it. They're as bound to us as we are to them. Maybe even more, for now."

The *for now* part was the bit that was going to come back to bite us, but there was no point in lingering on that.

There was nothing we could do to change it, after all.

"Alright," she sighed heavily.

Her dog licked her face and snuggled up closer, so she scratched his head softly.

"Goodnight," I murmured, grabbing my suitcase. "You guys will have more space now, at least."

She scooted over a bit as I hauled my suitcase across the house.

In our room, Auden pointed to the closet, so I set my stuff in there before heading back to the ladder, excited to try to get some actual sleep now that I wasn't sharing a bed with anyone.

CHAPTER 15

I WOKE UP TO AN EARTHQUAKE.

Or a jerk of a merman making the earth quake, at least.

My head jerked up off the pillow, my gaze moving rapidly around the space as I tried to figure out how bad the earthquake would be. It only took half a second to notice that Auden was shaking my bed; not an earthquake.

False alarm.

"We have to keep going with the power transfers if you're going to get a portal open," Auden growled at me.

"Good morning to you too," I muttered, scrubbing an arm over my eyes as a yawn stretched my face. "Do you even sleep?"

"Not well, when there's a woman snoring above me."

That was fair. I'd snored since I was a kid; my grandpa had always said that it was a sign that I was sleeping well. I didn't think that was true, but nothing I'd tried had stopped the snoring, so I'd accepted it as a part of life.

"Snoring is a sign of health in humans," I lied.

At least that much of me hadn't changed when I turned into a faery. Or *as* I changed into a faery, since according to my lovely husband, I was still in the process of changing.

"Sure it is," Auden drawled.

He disappeared, the door shutting harder than it needed to as he left the room.

"Annoying fae," I muttered.

"I heard you," he called out from the other side of the door.

Ignoring him, I climbed down the ladder and walked over to my bag, then started digging through it. Pulling out the one-piece swimsuit I had yet to try on, I shucked my clothes and wormed my way into it. Peeing was difficult in a one-piece, but everything else I had still needed to be washed, so I'd have to deal. The swimsuit had an excessive number of cutouts, but I didn't care.

After tugging one of my big, worn *Tom's Garage* shirts over the suit, I braided the ridiculous mass of hair, and left the room holding the tail-end of the braid. So far, I'd been leaving my hair down so I didn't accidentally give myself an eyeful of the points at the tops of my ears, because that freaked me out even more than the insanely-large hair.

Six male eyes tracked me to the bathroom, and I flipped the kings my middle finger as they stared at me. The door slammed behind me, and I grabbed a hair-tie before my eyes met my ears.

Halting there, I just... stared.

Nope, still not used to my new appearance.

The braid unraveled quickly, leaving my pale waves in weird shapes. I grabbed a brush and tugged it through the masses, muttering curses at every one of the many tangles.

By the time I was done brushing, I resembled an electrocuted poodle, but left the room with a sigh.

It was pointless.

I didn't look like me; I didn't even really feel like me. What did it matter if I couldn't tame my hair?

Hearing the muffled sounds of the other two girls talking quietly in my old room, I knocked twice before stepping inside. "How are you doing?" I checked, looking between them.

"Glad we don't have to do more power transfers." Hannah shrugged. "How are you?"

I pointed at my electrocuted-looking hair. "This well."

Both girls grinned.

"November," Auden barked from the living room.

"I swear, he thinks he's my prison guard," I grumbled, giving them a quick wave. "I can show you to the cafeteria after this if you want."

The girls eyes lit up.

"There's a cafeteria?" Elyn asked.

"Yup."

"Let's do it," Hannah agreed.

"It's a date." I slipped out of the room.

The other girls would probably get propositioned like I had, but I was sure they could take it. And since we could still lie, they could always claim to be sleeping with their kings too. Although, I wasn't sure if they could pull it off. They both seemed pretty damn genuine.

Auden, the other kings, and I headed out to the beach.

"Where's Ien?" I checked.

"Trying to see the outcome of us allowing our queens to move in with you," Kalus said easily. I didn't know why he'd given the information so readily, and wasn't sure I liked it. But I'd go with it.

My eyebrows raised. "Seriously?"

"Yup."

"How do his visions work?" I checked.

"An answer for an answer," Kalus said, shooting me a grin.

"Eh. I'm in enough question-debt to Auden as is. I'll pass." I glanced at the sea king, and his stony expression. "Let's get this over with."

He handed me the knife.

The scars already went up and down his entire left arm, and most of his right. I imagined we'd move to his chest or abdomen when we filled his arms, since he seemed to want the scars spaced out, though I'd never been given a real explanation for that.

Or much else, really.

"We're doing two today," Auden growled at me. "Here, and here," he gestured to his forearm just below his elbow, and then to his chest.

My eyebrows raised again. "Seriously? You almost passed out last time, and we only did one."

"I was fine."

Yeah, right.

Whatever. If he wanted to pretend to be a tough guy, that was his call.

"Voll," he barked.

I stared at one of my non-sneaky guards, who came striding out of the ocean, rich orange hair dripping water down his face and shoulders.

Was he a merman too?

"Keep an eye on things," Auden ordered, before turning to me. "Lets' go, Noa."

He seemed to use my full name, which I wasn't a huge fan of, and my nickname, which I preferred, interchangeably. Which annoyed me. Not enough to argue about it again, though. We argued enough as it was.

I grabbed his hand in one of mine, positioning his arm as his fingers clenched around mine. We'd taken to doing that before I cut him, and it made me feel slightly better about the whole disturbing ritual.

At least he was holding on to me for support, not just despising me for hurting him. Though I wouldn't blame him if he hated me.

The first one was quick and clinical. My stomach still turned a bit, but I was getting used to the blood and everything.

But my throat swelled as I put the knife to his chest. He already looked a bit dizzy; I didn't want to knock the guy out. Sure, I wasn't his biggest fan, but I didn't hate him. He'd protected me, and fed me, and clothed me. Despite his shitty attitude, he was far from the monster I'd assumed him to be when we met.

"Are you sure?" I checked.

His glare answered the question.

I pulled my extra hand from his, and set my palm on his chest as I went up on my tiptoes to give myself better access. Cutting his arms had been difficult enough to talk myself into; cutting his chest would be worse.

I lifted the knife, trying to ignore the catch in my throat and the clench in my abdomen.

Crap. I didn't know if I could do it.

Auden's hand grabbed mine, and like he had on that first day, he moved my hand and the knife for me.

Curses I didn't understand poured from his lips as I planted my hand over the injury. It bled profusely though; a lot more than the other ones had. My nausea grew as his chest grew slippery beneath me.

Without warning, Auden tipped.

He fell backward, his hands on my wrists as he held my palms to him, and we both crashed to the sand. My head cracked against the center of his freakin' hard chest, and I panted as for the first time, I *felt* it.

The magic.

Auden's magic, slipping into me through my hands. Through the cut in his body.

"Holy shit," I breathed.

The ocean waves washed over my ankles, and I propped myself up on Auden's chest as his wound finally started to heal.

He looked so out of it that I felt terrible.

The waves rose to my calves.

"That must be a little over half," Merzo murmured.

My gaze jerked to the sky king. "Half of what?"

The ocean washed up the backs of my thighs, and though the kings didn't answer, I knew.

I had taken over half of Auden's magic.

The water slipped backward as panic clutched me.

"*Wist*," Kalus muttered. He streaked across the sand, running into the house. Merzo was just behind him, as a shadow rose over me.

I glanced backward in time to see a massive wave rushing toward us, and grabbed onto Auden's body. He wasn't unconscious, but he may as well have been, and no matter how much of a bastard he was, I couldn't abandon him to the rush of the waves.

The ocean crashed into us.

Our legs bumped, shifting to tails as I held onto Auden as if our lives depended on it. The slide of scales on scales was strange, but not our biggest problem.

The water threw us around until I couldn't tell up from down or left from right, my mind spinning.

Auden's arms finally engulfed me. He didn't speak—I doubted we could underwater—but when my panicked gaze met his steady, angry one, it calmed me a little.

His eyes grew hard, his jaw clenching as the water tossing us around began to slow.

When it came to a standstill, his jaw finally relaxed, and he swam us downward—or up, maybe?

We reached the surface and his arms remained locked around me as I inhaled air, feeling my scales retreat to wherever they always went.

"Why did that happen?" I asked Auden, voice shaking a bit. I wasn't a control freak, but I hated being thrown about by nature as much as anyone else.

"You now hold the majority of the power, so the oceans respond to you above all others." His voice was strained.

"But it's your power," I protested.

"Which is why I was able to calm it," he agreed, bite in his voice. "But a few more transfers, and you'll have to do it yourself."

Calm the ocean myself? I hadn't even been able to tell up from down.

"You didn't warn me about this." My voice shook more, then.

"I'm not your damned father. Figure the magic out like the rest of us." He let me go.

The ocean held me up, keeping my head above the water, and there was a flash of silver as Auden dove down and vanished into the depths of the ocean.

Diving after him frantically, my eyes jerked back and forth as I searched the waves for the fae.

He was gone.

I surfaced again—since the waves had calmed a bit and my head had stopped spinning, I could tell up from down once more.

Turning my head in both directions, I looked for land.

Avalon Island?

It was gone.

Where was I?

Had Auden really just let the ocean carry me out into the middle of nowhere, and then abandoned me?

"What the hell?" I yelled after the merman, knowing he was too far gone to hear me.

He had ditched me.

"Dammit!" I swore at the sky.

The ocean began to churn around me.

"Crap." My eyes dropped to the water moving around my chest. It grew choppier by the moment. "This is not good. Really, really not good. Auden?" I yelled his name again, growing panicked as the waves started to sway hard enough to move me around with them. "Chaos!" I cried out in desperation, just before the water tugged me under.

A lungful of water entered my nose, and although my legs became a tail, the feel of it only enhanced my fear and anger.

The water's current grew stronger, dragging me deeper, and I was entirely at its mercy.

CHAPTER 16

THE OCEAN MUST'VE THROWN me around for hours before it finally tossed me back to the surface. My head popped up above the water, and I sucked in air. It cleared my lungs, closing my gills and leaving me with my two sad, exhausted feet kicking viciously as I tried like hell to stay up.

My panic had abated over a long, long time, as hopelessness replaced it.

Another wave formed, and with it the ocean sent me spinning, rolling through the water until I rolled up over the edge of the waves and crashed face-first into the sand.

My eyes burned, and I coughed up water and sand together.

"Come on, ocean," I mumbled into the sand.

"It merely responded to your emotions," Auden's voice said, from somewhere off to my side.

I didn't even have the energy to jump or scream. "Of course you're here."

He didn't respond to that, and I wondered if I'd imagined him up.

After a couple hours of ocean-tornado hell, it wouldn't even be surprising.

"Are you going to pout there all day, or can we go now?"

Apparently he wasn't just a figment of my imagination.

"If one of us likes to pout, it's not me," I muttered back.

A pair of gigantic hands grabbed me by the waist, lifting me up into the air. I screamed as he chucked me out into the water, and the scream morphed as water refilled my lungs.

It was too bad my gun wasn't waterproof; shooting Auden was starting to sound really freakin' good.

He appeared beside me in the water, and when the ocean-tornado kicked back up, he seemed to be guiding it.

WE LANDED on the beach at Avalon Island in the middle of the afternoon.

I could've sworn more time had passed while I'd been out there, lost to the ocean.

He stood beside me on the beach while I coughed up sand and misery, my stomach empty but churning and my mind absolutely exhausted.

"You're a real bastard," I snapped at Auden.

All he said before disappearing was, "Control your magic."

Hannah and Elyn came out of the house while I sat on my hands and knees and rinsed my mouth with more ocean water. It didn't taste gross to me anymore, and I was trying to get rid of the rest of the sand on my tongue and between my teeth. I'd need to floss, but that would require going inside the house, where Auden was. And considering I wanted to shoot him, that wasn't a great idea.

"Damn," Elyn whistled at me.

"Don't start." I crawled out further, tilting my head forward as I tried to scrub all the sand off my scalp and out of my mass of hair.

"You looked like you just hiked through a wet haboob," Hannah remarked.

I snorted. "Haboob? What is that, another fae curse?"

She grinned. "No; it's a sandstorm."

"Liar."

"I swear, they're real. And that's their real name."

"I call bullshit," Elyn shot back. "No way in hell would some scientist name a sandstorm that."

"I don't know where the term came from, but I swear, it's real. I'd look it up and show you if our phones hadn't been stolen." Hannah said, though excitement died down at her mention of the fae kings.

Their kings had stolen their phones?

Damn.

"Stop reminding me that Auden isn't as much of a jerk as he seems," I grumbled at them, standing up and flipping my hair back into place. That stuff weighed as much as Hannah's dog, I swear. "Let's go to the cafeteria."

Really, I just wanted to get away from Auden. Which wasn't likely to happen, since he needed to stay near me. But he'd proved that staying near me didn't necessarily mean he would be visible, when he'd followed me around while the ocean beat the shit out of me.

Even though I felt at peace in the water, my body hurt from the constant pounding and moving. And my brain felt like someone was driving a nail through it, too.

I just wanted to go home, take some Tylenol, play my piano for a few minutes, and go to bed.

But between the end of the world and the fae-marriage-nightmare I'd gotten roped into, what I wanted was no longer possible.

Elyn offered me a hand, tugging me to my feet, and then we all started off toward the main part of the sea castle.

I pointed out the few sites I knew in the castle as I led them to the cafeteria. We definitely had eyes on us, but that was a given—and I was pretty sure my guards, Voll and Ered, were tailing us fairly close.

"Did the kings try to hurt you while I was gone?" I asked the other women as we walked.

They exchanged grimaces. "No." Hannah spoke first. "They tried to get us to go back to their castles, but still wouldn't tell us anything. We barely managed to convince them not to whisk us away."

"Hopefully I can get the portal open soon so we can get them back to Avalon," I said tiredly.

The girls exchanged looks.

I didn't want to know what it was about this time.

"Have you thought about what we're going to do after the portal's open?" Elyn finally asked, choosing her words carefully.

No.

I hadn't.

We'd talked about the fact that they'd probably try to kill us, and that they'd probably take us to Avalon too, but worrying about that hadn't seemed like a priority.

I shook my head wordlessly.

"At least the Earth will be safe from them," I said, not wanting to have to really think about what the future held.

"We'll most-likely end up trapped in Avalon, Noa," Elyn said. "Where they wiped out all of the other women, for reasons they still won't tell us. And for all we know, that portal will be a one-way trip."

Well, that wasn't *wrong*.

"I never thought we'd be going back home." I gave her a shrug as we approached the cafeteria. "Everything fell apart when the fae appeared anyway; going to a new world won't be much different than coming to this one was." I gestured toward the island around us.

"Except that they'll try to kill us," Hannah countered.

I shrugged. "It feels like they're already doing that."

"Have you seen those guys?" she checked. "They're massive. If they were trying to kill us, we'd know."

That was probably true.

"We need to think of a way to become indispensable. We need them to need us," Elyn said. "I for one don't want to die five minutes after being dragged into a new, magical world."

"We'll think on it while we eat," I told her.

Truthfully, I was hoping the other women would just

forget after we had food, so I could go take a nap. I was exhausted.

The fae in the food line cleared as we approached, and the other girls looked surprised. Grabbing plates, we walked down the serving line. As always, the fae serving the food bobbed their heads in silent bows, murmuring about what a pleasure it was to serve the queens, and we headed to a table that looked to have been recently evacuated just for us.

We sat down, and three other fae men immediately filled the empty seats at the table.

None of them looked at me; all three focused on the redheads beside me.

And I was pretty sure I recognized at least one of them as one of the guys who had tried to convince me to invite him into my bed.

Though I didn't condone cheating, my lips twitched as I fought a grin.

More propositioning was definitely about to go down.

"Beautiful women," one of the fae purred.

I coughed back a snort, and the fae looked at me with concern.

"I'm fine." I waved off their worry. "Ate some sand earlier."

Confusion mingled with their concern.

Most sea fae probably didn't end up with their faces in the sand often; I had Auden and the ocean to blame for that *fun*.

"What are your names?" Hannah asked, her voice polite. I knew she'd met some of the friendlier fae, and wasn't entirely against all of them the way Elyn seemed to be. But Elyn had been locked in the sky castle, so I didn't blame her for feeling that way. Hell, it was probably smarter anyway.

The men rattled off their names, and I shoveled mashed potatoes into my mouth like I was starving.

Whoever was in charge of making the menu seemed to have a thing for mashed potatoes—or they realized that I did, and were hoping they could sweeten me up with potatoes to talk me into letting *them* into my bed.

It wouldn't happen, but I'd definitely keep enjoying the potatoes.

"What do you require, in exchange for bedding me?" a purple-haired fae asked. I couldn't tell if he was addressing Hannah or Elyn—and I didn't think they could tell either.

I couldn't hide the choking laugh that time.

Wow, the fae were terrible at this.

Elyn and Hannah looked at each other, and then looked at me. "Did he really just ask us that?"

My head bobbed.

Maybe I should've given the cheating lecture that day instead of lying about having sex with Auden.

Whoops.

Too late.

Now I understood why becoming a recluse outside of work wasn't recommended by doctors anywhere; realizing that this conversation would come back up and telling the truth instead would've been wise.

The fae with purple hair who had spoken earlier, added,

"You're at odds with your husbands. Should you sleep with us, they'll feel pain, and it'll encourage them to do better."

Wait, what?

No one told me that part.

"What?" I leaned over the table, eyes narrowing. "I thought it was supposed to be an insult."

"It is; the magic in the wedding bond causes them physical pain, on top of it."

What the hell was wrong with these people?

"I'm so glad I'm not a real faery," Hannah muttered, slouching against her chair. "What if the fae slept with other women?"

The fae blinked. "The same would happen to you. But men don't cheat."

I scoffed at that bullshit. I didn't know the ratio of cheating men to women, but I was pretty sure it was either even or weighted toward the men.

"None of us are sleeping with any of you," Elyn told them, standing up and leaning over the table. "If we're horny, we'll find human men to take care of us so we don't need to deal with you and your politics."

The fae stood up, jewel-toned eyes flashing in challenge. "A fae will do much better than a human in your bed."

I glanced up as the sky darkened a bit, and then looked around for Merzo.

Elyn hadn't taken half his magic yet, had she?

"You've got no way to back that up, do you?" Elyn taunted.

She was usually pretty quiet, so apparently this guy had really pissed her off.

"One kiss, and I'll prove it."

Thunder cracked overhead, and all of our eyes jerked upward.

"We should go," Hannah said, standing up.

Elyn stepped away from the table and put a hand on her hip as she faced off with the fae, ignoring Hannah. "You think you can rock my world with one kiss? Prove it."

This...was not good.

Elyn looked annoyed, but she didn't seem angry.

And the darkening skies... they looked angry.

Which meant Merzo was behind them.

Which meant he was probably watching everything that was happening.

CHAPTER 17

—————

"OH, I WILL." The purple-haired fae strode over to Elyn. His hands cupped her cheeks.

"We should stop this," Hannah whispered to me, fidgeting uncomfortably as we stepped away from the table and walked a bit closer to Elyn. I didn't know what was going to happen, but with the sky storming, I was getting out of the way.

"She's a grown woman."

And I didn't think Merzo would let it happen, TBH.

But I was interested enough in seeing if he did.

Because if he naturally felt possessive over Elyn despite their lack of conversation and connection and pretty much anything else... well, I might have some insight into why Auden was so angry all the time.

Pink-Hair's mouth moved toward Elyn's.

A breath before their lips touched, lightning cracked down between them, and they flew apart.

Pink-Hair was launched through a dozen tables, crashing through stone and wood and food and fae.

Elyn shot backward, flying toward the food line, but Merzo caught her with a loud grunt before she'd gone more than a few feet.

"What the hell?" she yelled at him, spinning awkwardly in his arms as her feet found the ground again. Her palms hit his chest, and surprisingly enough, he teetered and then moved back a few steps.

Taking her with him, of course.

"If you're giving a fae a chance to prove we can change your mind with a kiss, it'll be me," Merzo growled.

"Yeah, right. Why would I kiss the husband I didn't choose, who's planning on *killing me*?"

"That's the plan, but that doesn't mean *I'm* planning on it."

"Same thing."

Okay, I was definitely curious now.

"No. It's not." He paused. "Killing you would effectively kill most of my soul because of our bond, Elyn. Ien warned us that we'll need to kill you to maintain peace, but maintaining peace in Avalon has never been anyone's priority."

Well, that was screwed up.

But not hard to believe, given all I knew about the fae.

"I don't believe you." She pushed him away with another blast of air, and that time, he released her.

"I can't lie," he said, lifting his hands up on either side of his head.

"I didn't hear you promise to protect me with your life,

or even *not kill me*," she shot back. "So why the hell would I trust you?"

He honestly looked surprised by what she'd said. "Because I'm your husband."

Clearly that meant *everything*, considering the marriages were so arranged that we'd been tricked into signing the marriage licenses and/or certificates.

"That means almost nothing to me." Elyn shook her head, turning and stalking back toward our table.

She stopped when she saw the plates and table, smashed and tossed everywhere.

"I can still rock your world," the purple-haired fae said, walking back to Elyn unsteadily.

"Go suck a lemon," Hannah muttered under her breath, and I snorted.

The blast of lightning that threw the fae returned again —harder, and further— and cut me off mid-snort. The flirty fae flew backward once more, and the awful crack as his body collided with the wall was enough to make anyone sick.

Hannah gagged, falling to her knees and vomiting up however much of her dinner she'd managed to get down. I held her hair back, trying not to puke myself.

"What the hell?" Elyn shrieked at Merzo. "You can't just kill people!"

"He's fae. His body will regenerate and he'll come back," one of the other men told her.

She didn't take her glare off Merzo.

Hannah tried to get up, and I eased her up onto her feet.

Her face was pale, and her hand was over her mouth as she remained standing.

"Grab her some water," I told one of the fae beside me.

He slipped away immediately, though I didn't know if he was running away from me or actually getting her water.

Merzo tried to grab Elyn again, and then the strangest thing happened.

A group of the sea fae surged between her and the king, cutting him off from her.

Fury shone in his eyes, and I tackled Hannah to the ground—away from the vomit—expecting the biggest lightning bolt yet.

But it didn't come.

"Get off my land before I drown your sorry ass," Auden snarled at the sky king.

The air grew electric as the power between the two men swelled. I kind of wished I had control over my power, then, so I could throw down with the kings.

Lightning cracked down toward Auden, but water gathered above the sea king's head as if out of nowhere, and the lightning slammed into that instead.

The water exploded. Hot droplets flew everywhere, and I blocked Hannah with my own body. But, when the hot water hit my skin, it barely felt warm.

It was insane.

When I remembered that the deep ocean water hadn't felt cold... and that my showers hadn't felt hot, either, everything made a bit more sense.

I was a mermaid; part fish.

And at least partially cold-blooded, apparently.

Auden didn't waste any more time.

The water gathered itself again, and formed a spear. Within seconds, it shot through the air and pierced straight through Merzo's chest.

The sky king staggered backward as the water spilled down his body, mixing with his blood.

Elyn screamed, clutching at her chest like she was the one dying.

"Tell me he's going to resurrect," I mumbled to Voll, who had appeared beside me and Hannah when the lightning-water-explosion had gone down.

A wave crashed into the side of the building, but no one seemed to notice.

Merzo's body vanished.

"He'll reappear in the center of the island within an hour or two, healed," Voll confirmed.

Well, that was something.

The sea fae started setting their tables back up, as if that whole thing hadn't just happened. Elyn was still holding her chest as if she was in pain, and staring in shock at the spot Merzo had occupied.

Auden's eyes flashed across the room. "No one touches the human women without their permission." He didn't yell, but the threat hung heavy in the air.

A wave crashed against the side of the building, and everyone's attention snapped to Auden.

Except his.

He just looked at me.

The next wave hit harder.

The sea fae started murmuring back and forth; worrying Auden was out of control?

He crossed the cafeteria in a few strides, and I knew what was coming.

Scrambling backward, I shook my head at him.

His arms engulfed my waist, and he hauled me out of the cafeteria. As soon as we were out of the cafeteria's eyesight, he broke out into a run.

Another wave crashed against the castle, loud enough that there was no doubting that it was getting stronger.

Or wilder.

"You've got to stay calm," Auden growled at me, shaking the hell out of me as he sprinted back to the beach.

"You're never calm," I shot back. "The ocean didn't react this violently to you."

"What do you think caused all those wisting tsunamis?"

Reaching the edge of the castle, we found the water much higher than it should've been.

"Calm yourself," he snarled again.

"How?" I demanded.

"How should I know what would calm you?"

Freakin' fae.

He launched me toward the water like I was a football, rather than a person, and a scream left me as I crashed into the ocean.

It whisked me out into the sea, once again sending me spinning and tumbling wildly. My tail reappeared, though it was useless while the ocean threw me around like I was nothing more than a strip of seaweed.

Once again, Auden was nowhere to be seen.

And the ocean was just... angry?

Or afraid?

I wasn't even sure what emotions I'd been feeling when all of that had happened.

Apparently, it wasn't anything good, though.

The ocean's constant spinning and moving exhausted me pretty rapidly, and when I was drop-dead tired, it finally started to slow. And eventually, stopped.

I floated up toward the surface, my eyes scanning the open ocean around me. There were no fish nearby that I could see; they were probably smart enough to swim away from the insanity that was the water around me.

Auden swam into view, and I gave him the angriest look I could muster while so exhausted I could've passed out in the water itself.

He was gorgeous, with his silvery-white tail and those insane muscles. The white t-shirt plastered to his chest only made him look more attractive, somehow.

We both surfaced, and I started to tread water when my tail became legs.

"Stop throwing me into the ocean," I tried to yell, but I was so exhausted that it came out sounding like I wasn't even annoyed.

"Stop losing control of your emotions," he shot back.

"Seriously? Coming from you? When are you not angry?"

"Anger helps me control my other emotions."

"Anger isn't an emotion you can hide in," I argued. "Anger is big, and heavy."

"Believe me or don't," he growled. "You're the one putting your world at risk of more tsunamis."

The ocean dragged me off again as panic took hold in my chest, and I was lost to the waves.

I WASN'T sure how much time passed before the ocean finally spat me out. It felt like forever, but was probably only another hour or two.

The water tossed me up onto a sandy beach like it had earlier, and didn't bother peeling myself off the ground right away. Auden would inevitably show up, lecture me, and toss me back into the sea anyway. Last time, I hadn't even gotten to look around and see where I was before he'd chucked me back in.

After a few minutes passed in silence, I was tired of breathing in sand and seawater, and lifted my head up off the shore.

My eyes scanned the space.

The island was smaller than my apartment back in Nebraska, boasting nothing but a couple of jagged rocks and a few inches of sand.

Where was I?

My gaze dipped to the water and I studied it, looking for a flash of silvery-white that would give away the man following me around.

I didn't see him, though experience told me he was probably nearby anyway. He'd said that it felt like being ripped apart when he was far away, after all.

Rolling over, I sat down on my ass on the beach and stared out at the ocean. It was dark outside, but I could make out the ocean fine thanks to whatever had changed in my eyes when I became a faery. The waves weren't calm, by any definition of the term, but I didn't see anything that made me think a tsunami was building. And that had to be a good sign, didn't it?

I MUST'VE SAT THERE for twenty minutes before the waves started to grow choppier.

The wind could've been to blame... but my emotions were much more likely.

I'd realized that I was completely alone, with no way to get back to Avalon Island. If Auden hadn't followed me, I was probably going to die on a chunk of rock and sand.

I remembered my tail, and calmed down a bit.

"I could probably get myself somewhere," I told the ocean. "I'm kind of a mermaid."

Although I had a tail, I couldn't really call myself a full mermaid because I didn't know anything about being one. Was there a way for me to navigate while I was underwater? Was there some kind of innate fish-magic that I now possessed?

Little girls everywhere dreamed of becoming what I was,

but my tail hadn't come with any kind of magical happiness or a talking fish companion. I was still just me.

"I never dreamed of being a mermaid," I told the ocean. "I wanted to be a princess astronaut, and my grandparents convinced me it was a reasonable life goal."

The memory made my throat swell.

They had always believed in me. No matter what I'd wanted to become, they had told me I could achieve it as long as I worked my ass off to do so.

Why else would I have made music and posted videos nearly every day for the past three years? Posting things on the internet without knowing whether or not they would succeed was stressful. No matter what I tried or how hard I worked, there were always people who had larger audiences or more fans, and that hurt like hell.

But I knew what I wanted to be.

And I had believed that I would get there, eventually.

And now that the fae had come, that dream was gone.

Maybe the internet would pick back up eventually. Maybe people would go back to watching videos. Maybe they would even watch *my* videos now that my name was probably plastered all over the news as one of the girls who'd married one of the fae.

But I'd been sacrificed to the fae, forced to become the sea queen, and that life I'd wanted so badly was over.

"Everyone has dreams," I whispered to the ocean. It was something my grandpa had said to me a thousand times. "The only people who reach them are the ones who work their asses off until those dreams come true—and continue working their asses off afterward."

Tom's Garage had been his dream, and he had made it a success. Thousands of reviews had praised him for the hard work and honesty of his business. He had never really retired; even when he was told he had cancer, given only weeks to live, he hadn't given up the garage until he was satisfied that he'd found another guy who would love the business as much as he did.

Before the fae came, I thought I had time. We all did, I guess. I pushed through the pain of losing the last member of my support system, I worked my ass off, and at least most of the time, I loved the music I created. Not having as much success as I'd wanted was the hard part.

"But that's over now," I murmured to the waves.

They were a little choppier than before, but the water didn't seem to have risen.

"At least I won't have to hurt over internet strangers who don't like my music anymore."

The ocean didn't answer, of course. But I felt like maybe it was listening, somehow.

Kalus had a piano in his house; maybe I could bring it to Auden's.

And maybe I could bring it to Avalon, too.

Maybe, even if my dream was over, I could still have my music.

The thought wasn't entirely hopeful, but it wasn't entirely full of despair, either.

"There are worse things to be than alone," I reasoned with myself. "I could be a complete bitch. Or a criminal. I could've run from the fae—forced some other poor girl to take my place. That would definitely be worse. And really, I'm not completely alone. I have Elyn and Hannah. It hasn't been long enough to really get to know each other, but maybe we could become family."

I remembered the way Elyn had screamed and clutched at her chest when Merzo temporarily died.

Our connections to the kings had to be stronger than they'd explained; stronger than we'd realized. They kept shit from us all the time, though, so that wasn't exactly surprising.

"And in a way," I said, my voice lowering to barely above a whisper. Just in case a certain blond someone was listening in on my little chat with myself and the ocean. "I have Auden, too. He's not much of a talker, and he doesn't seem to like me much, but from what I've gathered, he's as trapped in all of this as I am. And that's got to count for something, right?"

Yeah, maybe I was losing my mind a bit. But there were worse things than losing my mind, too.

Like... being sacrificed to the fae.

But it was a little late to avoid that.

I stared out at the ocean for a bit.

My grandpa hadn't been a judgy man. If someone dressed strangely, he'd say they were "a character". If someone made choices he didn't agree with, he'd shrug and remark, "it's their life, not mine". And if I was grumpy or angry, he'd just leave me to my anger and remark that he hoped I had a better day tomorrow.

He'd always told me that most people weren't bad—they just made bad decisions sometimes. That I wasn't moody or grumpy; I was just thinking and dealing with my emotions the best I could.

He'd understood that I was introverted, and that I kept quiet when I was hurting instead of letting the world see my emotions.

When my boyfriend and I broke up right before I started college, and I didn't cry over him, I told my grandpa that I thought I was broken. He'd given me a hug, and said that if the world made me think I was broken for dealing with my emotions in my own way, it was the world that needed a tune-up.

And... Auden did seem to be trying, in his own odd, angry way. He cooked for me, and bought me clothes, and protected me and the other girls.

Maybe *he* was just dealing with his emotions in his own way.

Getting dropped in a new world where the ocean itself reacted to your emotions couldn't have been easy, after all.

I made up my mind not to be angry with him for his anger.

And hey, maybe if I wasn't a bitch to him, eventually we could become friends. As gorgeous as he was, and despite our husband-wife relationship, I couldn't really see us as anything more than friends. But friends, sure.

Tired of staring out at the ocean, I lowered myself to my back on the rocky sand and stared up at the stars.

Wonder touched me as I looked at the sky. I'd never seen so many stars before, and I'd never seen them so clearly, either. It could've been because of my new eyes, but I doubted it.

I was pretty sure it had to do with being out in the middle of nowhere, away from everything and everyone.

Staring up at the stars, I finally let the craziness of everything that had happened in the past week—the past month, really—hit me.

The fae had destroyed the world as I knew it.

My dreams had up and vanished with the tidal waves, earthquakes, and storms.

I'd been chosen to marry one of the fae kings—chosen as a human sacrifice.

My body had changed.

I grew a tail and could breathe water.

And now, my emotions controlled the seas.

Nothing about what had happened was easy, or simple, but it was what it was. I'd cope with it, in time. It was just a lot to take in at the moment.

My arms wrapped around my stomach.

I should've been cold because of the soft breeze blowing over the tiny island I sat on, and my wet swimsuit clinging to my skin, but I wasn't.

And though I didn't cry, I let everything blow over me like the wind. The water lapped at my feet, slowly rising up until it covered all but my face.

CHAPTER 18

MY HAIR TANGLED with the sand around me, and I closed my eyes. Anger may have worked for Auden when it came to keeping his temper even, but that wasn't going to work for me.

I focused my mind on one of my favorite songs to play. It was a spin on *Hallelujah*, by Leonard Cohen, and it touched my soul in a way only music—and recently, the ocean —could.

My fingers moved in the sand as I played the notes I'd hit a thousand times, the music playing in my mind alone. Though my memory wasn't good enough that I could literally hear the music, I hummed the tune so softly that it was barely audible.

My emotions slowly began to calm, growing even as I played and replayed the song.

The words to it were hauntingly beautiful to me, and they ran through my mind as I hummed. My singing was terrible—I was about a thousand percent tone-deaf—but I could hum the tune decently enough to feel the impact of the music.

The ocean began to recede, slowly, and after a few run-throughs of *Hallelujah*, I slipped into my hummed rendition of *Viva la Vida* by Coldplay. It was another one of my favorites; the power-songs that calmed me and gave me goose-bumps and made me feel like I was on top of the world.

The water lowered back to my waist; it was working. My emotions were evening out, my feelings growing to a calm, quiet peace.

The next song was *First Day of My Life* by Bright Eyes, and the lyrics to that one really hit me hard.

My fingers carried me through *If The Story is Over* by Stratovarius before playing *Chasing Cars* by Snow Patrol.

Quiet sloshing noises met my ears as the water washed back beneath my toes, receding to where it was supposed to be. The sloshing had to be a person moving through the water; the ocean didn't slosh.

And I only knew one person who would be able to find me, at that moment.

"Good." Auden's approval was a bit shocking to hear.

"Thanks." My mind was still running over the last bit of Chasing Cars, trying to maintain the calmness I'd found so I could keep the ocean where it was supposed to be.

He offered me a hand, and I lifted an eyebrow at him.

"Is that you trying to help me? Color me surprised."

"Don't get used to it," he said, but didn't withdraw his hand.

I accepted it.

The calluses on his skin surprised me, given that he was a king, but I knew he'd only recently taken the throne. And that told me there was a lot about the man that I didn't know.

His grip was firm as he pulled me to my feet. "Are you going to follow me back in your mer form, or should I drag you again?"

"Eh, I think I'm going to stay here a while. Look; I've got the whole world to myself." I stretched my hands out at the sky.

"We need to be back there when Merzo resurrects." He shot me a warning look. "I don't trust the other kings."

That was good to know.

And also not good at the same time.

"I was kidding." I rolled my eyes as I stepped past him, wading back out into the water. I was a sandy, wet mess, and doubted even swimming fast with my tail would rid me of the sand on my scalp. I'd need a comb or something to do that. "I'll follow you, but I doubt I can swim as fast as you."

"In the stories, female sea fae were faster swimmers than the males," Auden remarked, passing me and diving into the water.

Huh.

He'd given me multiple pieces of information without me asking, or offering anything else in return.

That was new.

The words lingered in my mind as I followed him.

Surprisingly enough, it wasn't difficult to keep up with him. My body was adapting to being a faery, I guess.

If female sea fae were faster than men... maybe that had something to do with why mermaids were more common to hear about than mermen.

It seemed like a stretch, but maybe I was onto something.

The swim back was much faster than my unfortunate trip there, and not much time passed at all before we were striding up onto the shore of Avalon Island.

"Where's the center of the island?" I asked Auden.

"At the center of the island." He strode on ahead of me— on land, he was much faster than I was.

Jerk.

I followed him, pointedly not staring at his backside. He was my husband, but that didn't give me the right to perv on him when we'd both made it clear we weren't interested in being anything more than friends. As far as he was concerned, even being friends was too much.

My eyes skimmed the trees as we passed the gazebo and then reached the earth castle.

Auden led me down a trail around it, not slowing as we passed Kalus's home, and I continued following him as the trees grew thicker. The path was still worn, there, which told me it was used plenty frequently.

"How much further?" I asked Auden, ten or fifteen minutes after we'd passed the castle. My entire body ached thanks to both of my battles with the ocean, and I was exhausted.

He ignored me.

Back to being a bastard again, I guess.

I reminded myself that he was just having a shitty month, same as me. His terrible month was on a much, much different level than mine considering all of the tragedy he'd accidentally caused, but the idea behind it was similar.

And maybe tomorrow would be better for him.

We approached a small clearing less than a minute after I asked the question, and found Elyn sitting on the ground with her arms wrapped around her middle, her face pale and her gaze latched to some kind of *thing* in the middle of the clearing. Hannah sat beside her, and Kalus stood across from both of them, watching either the women or the *thing* in the middle. A few other fae were scattered around the clearing, all staring at the same thing or the women sitting by a tree.

I frowned as I tried to figure out what the thing in the clearing was. It was round, and a little bigger in diameter than Auden was, as well as white and ceramic-looking, almost, like... a big plate.

"What's that?" I whispered to Auden.

No response again, *shockingly*.

"It focuses the fae's energy to assist them in reforming," Ien explained from across the clearing, near Kalus. He looked less cheerful than usual, but still seemed happy.

Why he was happy while waiting for Merzo to reform or resurrect or whatever, I didn't know.

And why he was so much happier to give out information without me also sharing info, I didn't know either.

"Why do they need help resurrecting?" I asked.

"It's like a target," Ien said. "It gives a reformed soul and body a place to land."

"Why is it taking so long?" Elyn asked, her face pale.

Ien shrugged. "You have a decent amount of his magic. It's harder to reform with less magic."

Walking away from Auden, I headed over to the other women and dropped to my ass on the other side of Elyn. "You okay?" I asked her.

She gave me a tight smile. "It feels like someone has their fist wrapped around my heart."

"Not extremely pleasant, then," I remarked.

"No." She heaved a sigh. "Are you okay?"

"Me? Oh, I'm fine. Auden's magic is just difficult to control." And that reminded me... "Hey, Hannah?" I leaned forward a bit, so I could see her.

"Yeah?" She leaned forward too.

"Can I have your piano?"

Since none of the fae played, and neither of the other girls did either, I assumed she wouldn't be offended by the question.

"Sure." Her shoulders lifted. "Getting it over to the beach house will be a bitch, though."

"I'll bargain facts about my life with some of the fae." I glanced around the clearing, and found most of them staring back. "Although something tells me that since Elyn's opened the floodgates, most are going to want to bargain for a kiss."

The earth shook a bit, and all of us looked at Kalus.

His face was a neutral mask.

The moon above us darkened, and we all glanced up in time to watch dark clouds gather above our heads.

"He's coming," Ien announced.

Most of the fae in the clearing backed up a bit. I considered moving, but before I could, lightning cracked down onto the massive not-plate in the center of the space. A flash of light accompanied the lightning. When it faded to a bit of hazy smoke, Merzo was standing on the plate, naked and clutching at his chest.

Elyn inhaled sharply as he stepped off the plate. Her eyes closed, and her hand formed a fist on her chest as she began to breathe deeper than she had before.

"Better?" I asked her, as one of the fae took a pair of pants and a shirt to Merzo.

"Much better," she whispered, her eyes remaining closed as her fae king got dressed. "I hope you guys never have to feel that."

Yeah, same.

Merzo walked over to us, barely batting an eye at anyone else in the clearing.

He lowered to his knees in front of Elyn.

Feeling like I was intruding, I slid a foot or two to the side before standing up. Hannah joined me a few feet from the couple.

"I've never felt so much agony in the transitional place," Merzo murmured to Elyn. "I caused you pain."

"It wasn't the first time," she shot back, glaring at him. "You locked me in a damn library, while you were planning on killing me. That's not exactly romantic, is it?"

Merzo lowered his head a bit. "I'm sorry."

"You should be." She started to stand up, and he caught her arm quickly. When she pulled it out of his grip, he held both hands out to her.

"Please, let me help you."

"I don't want your help." She looked at Hannah and I, and we both saw her silent question. Hurrying to her side, we took her arms. "Let's go home."

I knew by "home" she meant the beach house. But I doubted she already considered it her home, which meant she was trying to test Merzo. Maybe even hurt him.

And I got that; he deserved it. It was her right to treat him however the hell she wanted.

But he had seemed genuine when he apologized a few moments ago.

The fae followed us back to the beach, and then through the sky as Elyn flew all three of us women to the house.

The flight was terrifying and I would've rather swam, but I got the feeling that Elyn needed the support. And I wasn't much as far as support went, but I could try.

When we made it back to the beach house, I grimaced as we walked in.

Everything was soaked. It didn't look like the water had risen more than a couple of feet—there was a water line on the walls—but it had definitely gone up, and almost to my waist.

I felt bad for Hannah's dog, but he ran up to us and jumped up on her, knocking her to the ground while she sputtered with laughter.

My heart sank as I stepped into my old room with the other girls. They shut the door while I went searching for my gun, and murmured quiet disappointment with me when I found my only source of protection completely ruined by the flood I'd caused.

Though I knew it was too late for the weapon, I tucked it glumly back under the mattress to keep it hidden from the kings.

Auden came in and used his power to dry everything before he stepped back out, gesturing for us to follow.

Back out in the mostly-bare living area, we found out that someone had left six plates overflowing with cafeteria food on the counter for us, and gratitude made my stomach rumble. I needed to find and thank whoever was responsible.

We ate in near-silence, then took turns in the bathroom, and headed to our rooms to sleep. Auden was already in the top bunk when I got there— leaving the bottom, much better bunk, open for me.

And whatever the reason he'd decided to take that bunk, I appreciated that he had.

CHAPTER 19

I KNEW the morning had come around when Auden shook my bed again. I groaned, rolling over and hitting him on the head. Not because I thought he was an alarm clock, like in old movies, but because I wanted to shut him up.

"When are you going to get used to waking up on time?" he grumbled at me.

"There's no clock, or alarm," I grumbled back. "So never, probably."

He scowled at me and left the room.

"Guess today's not his day either," I muttered to myself as I pulled on one of my cleanest-smelling swimsuits.

Still needed to do laundry.

Deciding I'd better not put it off any longer, I grabbed an armload of clothes and hauled it out to the living room.

"Where's your laundry machine?" I asked the two redheaded kings, since Auden was absent.

They both stared blankly at me.

"To wash clothes? Washer, dryer..." I trailed off, expecting them to figure out what I was talking about.

"There are fae assigned to wash clothes," they said, as if that should've been obvious to me.

That was someone's job?

Yikes. At least I wasn't the *laundry* Queen.

"Where do I find them?" I checked.

"You don't." Auden said, reentering the house. "Leave them in a pile by the door and I'll send the fae in for them."

I scoffed at him. "I'm not letting some horny fae dudes wash my underwear."

Auden's face twisted in a scowl.

"This may be the last power transfer we need to do," Ien tossed out, stepping into the room and flashing a bright smile at us. "And then, we'll be off to Avalon."

"Where you plan on murdering us," Elyn said, stepping out of the bedroom and crossing her arms.

Hannah stepped out with her. "We're going to stay here."

The kings didn't look convinced.

And considering that the couples couldn't really be apart, I understood why.

"It only takes one person to open the portal, right?" I glanced at Ien. I didn't like the guy, but he seemed like the most-likely source of answers. Whether or not said answers would be trustworthy was up in the air, even though they couldn't lie.

There were probably a dozen ways to get around that rule, too.

"Yes. But the other kings can't be away from their magic, and if Hannah and Elyn were to give it back, we don't know what would happen to any of them," Ien explained.

"Well we're definitely not giving it back without some kind of proof that we aren't going to get *murdered*," Elyn shot back.

"They won't kill you while you're holding their magic. To do so would permanently weaken them," Auden growled at the girls. "We'll figure out the rest of this after we're off this fae-forsaken planet and back in Avalon."

Yeah, today definitely wasn't a better day for him.

Figuring out the rest later didn't sound like a terrible idea though, assuming portals could go both ways. And though I doubted the fae would give me a straight answer if I asked about portals leading back to Earth, they had managed to get themselves to my planet. So why wouldn't they be able to get us back home after all of the king stuff was all said and done?

"Fine." Hannah's head bobbed in a nod. "Let's get this over-with."

We all shuffled outside.

"Two cuts again?" I asked Auden, assuming he was on-board with trying to get this done as fast as possible.

"Unless I can take more."

I was starting to think he had a death wish...or hated my planet even more than I realized.

Or maybe, both.

It was still strange to gather on the beach so everyone could watch me cut Auden, but I hoped I'd never get used to that. As soon as I did, I'd know there was something really, really wrong with me.

"Should we try the portal thing now, before we do this?" I asked Auden, gesturing to his chest and the knife in his hand.

"No."

"We tried yesterday. All it requires is your hair, and you shed it everywhere," Ien put in, waving toward the house.

My fingers caught the mess of waves tumbling down the front of me, fiddling with the strands for a moment.

They'd been taking my hair, using it to try to make portals, without me?

What the hell?

Auden put the knife in my hand, then gestured to his arm, chest, and then arm again. "Here, and then here, twice. We're aiming for four."

I bit my lip.

Two had pretty much knocked him out the day before; what made him think he could take four?

I still wasn't sold on cutting his chest to ribbons, either. The magic scars on his arms made him look tougher, but the chest one just made it look like he'd been attacked by a small animal or something.

"Can't we just rotate between arms?" I asked. "I really don't like this idea." I gestured to his chest with the hand not holding the knife.

"Switching locations ensures more power comes out. More blood, and therefore more magic, will come from his chest," Ien explained.

With a sigh, I stepped toward Auden.

His fingers tangled with mine, the hold platonic and meant to ward off pain as I lifted my knife to his bicep. My knife cut through his skin, and the front of my hip bumped his as I lifted my hand to his wound.

His hand found my waist, and gripped me hard as the blood leaked out of him, onto my skin. I felt like crap for hurting him, but there didn't seem to be any better option.

When that one was healed, I positioned my knife over his chest, just below the other cut, and grimaced.

This was really, really horrible.

His hand caught mine, and our eyes collided as he slashed through his own skin with my hand and knife.

His breathing was ragged as I covered the wound on his chest. He still gripped my hip tightly, but not tight enough to cause pain. And while I didn't much like being touched by a guy I wasn't interested in, letting him hold on to me to help him survive the pain was the least I could do.

And though I'd never felt it before, the rush of his magic slowly entering my blood or body—whatever faery part of me held that magic, was almost overwhelmingly strong.

By the time that injury closed up, he looked a bit dazed but still seemed determined.

"Again?" I asked, hoping he'd say no.

"Yes." The word was short and sharp, but I knew he wasn't being short to offend me. He was just in pain.

Muttering a curse under my breath, I cut him a third time.

His knees bumped mine, and his chest met mine as he

swayed a bit. I leaned back a little, trying to stay balanced and take some of his weight. I'd rather we not crash again, but he was in bad shape, so I'd probably survive the crash better than he did if we went down.

The wound healed, and he was sweating and panting as if he'd just finished running a marathon.

"Again," he tried to bark. It came out as barely more than a breath.

"I don't think that's a good idea," I warned. "We should probably just—"

"Again." He was angrier, that time.

Fine; it was his life, not mine.

I lifted my knife to his chest. His hands were iron on both my hips at that point; he wasn't going to help me at all.

With another curse under my breath, I cut him a fourth time.

He went unconscious before I could even press my hand to the injury.

Merzo shoved a hand forward, and my head jerked to the side in time to see him staring at me as I slapped my hand to the bleeding injury.

I really hated this—the cutting, the bleeding, the pain—but the rush of power was almost worse than that. It thrummed in my veins, and the ocean started to rock like a boat getting tossed in the waves.

It grew choppier and choppier as the power increased, thrumming harder and faster inside me.

It was getting stronger—starting to overwhelm me.

The world grew hazy as my fingers remained plastered to his chest.

I heard someone say, "We've got to calm her down."

"How?" someone else demanded.

"I don't know. He threw her in the ocean when she got worked up," a third person said.

They'd better not even consider—

A set of large arms wrapped around me loosely just before my feet left the ground. In one smooth motion, my body went flying toward the ocean, still wrapped in Auden's.

The ocean rose to swallow us, and my eyes slammed shut as the water dragged us downward. Our legs shifted to tails, but everything still felt really hazy and dizzying as we sank into the ocean, shimmering tails bumping while our chests remained plastered together.

We were tossed around for a while before my mind finally grew less hazy and I could blink my eyes and see clearly again.

The water slowed a bit as I looked around, taking in the darkness of the ocean. We seemed to be near the floor; I could see the bottom. That alone was enough to make my head spin again.

Plants I didn't recognize grew along the ground. It didn't look like soft sand, like we had on our islands, but like rough, sandy dirt. My nose wrinkled at the garbage I saw along the ground. Plastic water bottles, soda cans, garbage bags...

No wonder the ocean was so excited to listen to the fae's emotions. We took shitty care of it.

I glanced up at Auden's eyes and found him unconscious still. Why his arms were still holding me so tightly, I didn't know. But I was glad; I didn't want him to hurt because of the distance between us while he was so off his game, and I didn't want to be alone in the middle of the ocean, either. Because unlike him, I hadn't figured out whatever mermaid sonar I could use to find my way back to our temporary home.

Assuming that trying to wake him would be pointless, I wiggled around in Auden's arms until I managed to get free. Then, grabbing his beefy, scarred arm, I started swimming up toward the surface of the water. The currents were still moving faster than they probably should've been, but not fast enough to whisk me away even with a massive merman weighing me down.

It took a long time, and my lungs were burning when we finally reached the surface, but we made it.

Off in the distance, I saw a little island. It looked suspiciously like the one I'd sat on while giving myself a pep-talk the night before, so that was nice.

I dragged Auden over to the island. As we approached, I wished hard that the ocean could just give us a toss up toward the beach, like it had done for me the last few times.

And somehow, it listened.

A wave suddenly threw us up toward the beach, and we went rolling up the slight sand hill. Body-over-body, we crashed into each other a couple times on the way up the beach.

Right as we stopped rolling *up*ward, Auden's body went over mine and...teetered.

"Crap," I hissed, tugging him backward as he tipped.

He was too heavy though; we rolled right back into the ocean.

"Dammit!" I yelled before going under.

He grabbed me by the waist, suddenly, sitting up and dragging me up to a sitting position too.

I panted, watching him look around with his forehead knitted and wearing a disconcerted expression.

"Four is too many," I panted at him.

He blinked at me.

The ocean grew choppy once again, still responding to my mess of feelings.

That wasn't good.

Crawling up the sand, I collapsed on my face with my arms spread above me. My fingers pressed invisible keys as I forced myself to focus on an upbeat song I'd played for my grandpa a dozen times; *Count On Me*, by Bruno Mars. My mind rehearsed the words—or at least tried to, as I forced myself to focus.

I launched into a silent Bruno Mars marathon, guessing at the keys as I went through *Grenade*, *Just the Way You Are*, and *When I Was Your Man*.

CHAPTER 20

TEN SONGS LATER, I was sufficiently calm.

I lifted my head to see Auden staring out at the ocean, still looking a bit dazed.

"You good?" I asked him, trying unsuccessfully to wipe sand off my face with the back of my arm.

"No." His eyes didn't leave the horizon.

Well, what was I supposed to say to that? It was one of those questions that you asked just to hear someone lie about being fine.

"Maybe that was enough to get us to Avalon," I suggested, easing myself up to a sitting position.

"I doubt it. I'm sure Avalon will require every drop of my magic to recognize you as a faery."

He was telling me things?

Wow. I'd better take advantage of this situation.

"Why?"

"Magic is all or nothing. My magic, as a whole, is my personal imprint. Avalon is smart enough to see that you're only a fraction of a whole. And fae can portal out of Avalon without a problem, but only faeries can portal back home. It's why no one's visited earth in centuries, leaving us unprepared for the technological advances when we were dropped on our asses in your capitol."

I opened my mouth to tell him that they hadn't been in any of our capitols, but closed it because that information really didn't matter.

"Why were the faeries all killed?" I asked.

He didn't answer right away.

Was he waiting for me to share information too?

"No one knows. The records from that time were burned centuries ago, and all of the fae were reset shortly after."

Reset?

How did you reset a person?

"What does that mean?"

"In Avalon, when a fae is killed, he'll usually lose his memories and some of his power. Not his identity or personality, though, which is why we call it being *reset*."

My mouth formed an "O".

"Merzo remembered Elyn, though."

"She's his wife," he said simply. "And she carries much of his power. It holds his memories for him. He's not happy about the loss of power caused by my taking his life, though."

I'd noticed him avoiding Auden; that didn't seem like anger.

It seemed almost like fear.

"How much more powerful than them are you?" I asked.

He didn't answer.

"I can tell they defer to you, and one of the earth fae told me that you're a new king. So why do they look up to you?"

He remained silent once again, for a long moment, before he looked at me. Though I didn't look at him, I could feel his eyes on me. "What's this?" he finally asked, his fingers reaching for the ring on my neck around a chain.

I reached for it automatically, and he withdrew his fingers before our skin brushed. "My grandpa's wedding ring. It was the only material item with real meaning to him, and he told me he didn't want it buried in the ground when he died. I didn't want to lose it, so I put it on a chain."

Auden's expression was neutral, and I couldn't read in his eyes whether he was interested at all in this conversation. But since he was asking, I assumed/hoped he was. "Why not give it to one of his sons?"

"He only had one son. That son was married, but he didn't come around very often. I don't have any family other than my grandparents, either, so he thought that if I kept it, it would be a good way for me to remember that I wasn't alone."

Auden studied me, but I focused out on the ocean, waiting for him to answer me again.

"In Avalon, power is determined by how much land each type of fae possesses and holds. The sea fae are the only ones whose land doesn't change, so theoretically, we should be the most stable, powerhouse kingdom. But our problem lies in our leadership—as it always has. We've had nearly a hundred kings in the last three centuries, and as soon as we get a decent one, he's betrayed by someone who wants the throne."

He continued, "I was never interested in leading, but the king before me sold us out to the spirit fae. He's the reason we're here. I've been the strongest sea fae for a century, but I wasn't interested in playing the power struggle game so I never attempted to take the throne. My family finally convinced me, but I was too late. And here we are." He gestured out to the ocean. "On Earth." The disdain in his voice was clear. "You must've seen the garbage at the bottom of the ocean."

"Some people are too lazy to throw their stuff away." I paused. "But some fae try to kill each other just because they're bored, so I wouldn't say you're better than us."

"Death isn't permanent for us. Not anymore."

"Was it ever permanent?" I asked, curiosity seeping in.

"So the legends say. Given that our records were destroyed, it's hard to truly know."

Wow.

Look how much information I could get out of him when he was tired and not angry; I was on a freakin' roll.

"So are you going to try to kill me when we're back in Avalon?" I asked.

"I already ruined your life once by coming here. What's the point of ruining it again? Maybe if the faeries return to

Avalon, they'll be busy enough bedding each other to finally stop fighting."

It didn't pass my notice, the way he referred to fae as a whole that didn't include him. "That's not a real answer."

"No, Noa. I won't kill you—or even attempt to do so. Get me back home, and I'll make sure you stay alive for at least the first few years, so you have enough time to figure out how things work in my world."

That was fair.

"Do you think Kalus and Merzo are going to try to kill Hannah and Elyn?'"

He didn't answer.

More bargains? This was getting really old.

"My biological mom was engaged to my grandparents' son when I was conceived," I blurted. My story was complicated, but if telling it to him would get him to keep telling me important stuff, I'd spill the whole damn complicated mess of it. He already knew bits and pieces, but I just launched into the whole story.

"She cheated on him, and got pregnant with me by accident. She didn't believe in abortion, but she didn't want to keep the baby. When she started looking for a family for me, my grandparents were worried she and her questionable morals would pick the wrong family, so they asked to take me. It was easy, so she agreed."

My shoulders lifted. "So I'm not actually my grandparents' granddaughter. And I remind their son that his fiancée of three years cheated on him, so he's avoided me most of the time since I was born. Now that my grandparents are gone, I don't have anyone. But I have my memories, and everything they taught me—and they taught me a lot about life, and love, and dreams."

"I don't think Kalus and Merzo hate themselves enough to risk it." Auden knew it was his turn, and was paying up.

"What does that mean?"

"Do you recall the way Elyn acted when Merzo was temporarily gone?"

Yeah, that one would be hard to forget. "Of course."

"That feeling she was carrying would be permanent in any fae or faery whose spouse was fully dead."

"Wow. You'd better not die, then." I shot him a sideways glance.

It was still weird to think about the fact that he was my *husband*. That we had ended up with this permanent bond that we could never be free of, even in death.

Unless we *could* be free of it...

"Is there a way to undo a marriage?" I asked him.

He shot me a dark look, even with those bright eyes. "No. And the fae word for it is *kompeleno*, which loosely translates to *unbreakable companionship*."

"Not unbreakable *love*?" I asked, curious. I'd never learned another language, and thanks to the automatic-translate thing that had happened to me when I married Auden, it didn't seem like I'd need to.

"No. Love, by definition, is fickle. Companionship is not."

"I don't agree with that. Real love is steady, and trustworthy, and comforting. The way my grandparents loved each other... that's what real love looks like to me. It was just friendship, taken to the next level a dozen times over. They knew everything about each other, and loved each other because of all of that—the good, and the bad. And the way they laughed together..." I shook my head as the memories and emotions came rushing back. "I'd settle for a fraction of that friendship."

Auden looked at me a bit differently, after that, even though he didn't say anything. "I suppose they had a true *kompeleno*, then."

"I guess so."

Looking at him, I realized he had likely never seen a couple together. He had never even seen a woman until he came to Earth, so the chances of him seeing a couple interact were about zero.

"What are your friends like?" I asked him.

He stood, crossing his arms. "It's time we head back."

Dammit.

There went that wall again. His expression was stony and neutral, but it felt like something had changed a little between us. I didn't know a *lot* more about him, but I did know *more* about him. And he definitely knew more about me too.

I stood too. "Alright. Teach me how to navigate as a mermaid."

He scowled at me over his shoulder. "Teach yourself. That's the fae way."

"I'm not a fae, I'm a faery. And as it turns out, we faeries prefer to have someone explain things. Simply."

The look he shot me said he was not entertained by me.

He waded out into the water, diving in when it reached his waist, and I followed suit.

Keeping his pace wasn't difficult. Navigating, though... I was still clueless about how to do that.

CHAPTER 21

THE OTHER KINGS AND QUEENS—AS weird as that still was to say—were waiting on the beach when we got back. Hannah and Elyn sat together on the sand, their feet in the water, while Kalus and Merzo were leaned up against the wall of my beach house. The men looked like they might have been talking, but I doubted they'd say anything truly meaningful with the women there.

"You're alive," Kalus said, spreading his arms as I followed Auden to the shore. "I'm impressed."

"At least one of us is," Auden growled, heading inside.

"Want to hit the cafeteria?" I asked the other girls. "I know it's a bearer of bad memories, but the food..."

"Worth it," Hannah agreed, standing.

We both looked at Elyn.

She grimaced, glancing over her shoulder at the men as the redheaded brothers disappeared into the house after Auden. "Alright. It might be nice to talk away from them."

Hannah and I both nodded.

I was sure we wouldn't have long until they followed; with Auden's stronger connection to me, I doubted he'd be able to stay more than a room away from me without experiencing pain. Though, often, he seemed to ignore the pain for the sake of avoiding me.

Which was rude, but understandable. I'd do the same thing if I was in his shoes.

"So, I learned things," I declared to the other women.

We were a team, after all. And I was positive that Auden knew that whatever he told me about the fae, the other girls would also find out. I hoped he knew I'd keep quiet about the personal stuff, though. He hadn't *really* given me anything personal enough to keep quiet about, but if and when he did, I definitely knew how to keep my mouth shut.

I explained quickly the things I'd learned as we walked, even going so far as to explain the permanence of marriage and the unbreakable companionship thing. I couldn't remember the fae word for it, but I was sure we'd hear it again eventually, so that was fine.

They pestered me with questions I didn't have answers to as we reached the cafeteria, and we kept talking as we grabbed food.

This time, when we sat down at the single empty table, none of the other fae sat with us. It was both annoying, and a relief at the same time.

I wasn't interested in them obviously, or I wouldn't have bothered lying about sleeping with Auden. But I did still want to learn who they were and understand more about them. Plus, with less on the line, some of the non-royal fae might be more open-mouthed.

Voll and Ered caught my eye from across the cafeteria-clearing while I was eating, and I waved them over.

They glanced at each other, as if they were trying to figure out if I was calling for them.

Who else would I be waving to?

"Be right back," I told the other women, heading over to the soap-maker fae who I was 99% sure had recently been promoted to queen-guard duty. "Hey, guys." I grinned at them as I approached.

"Hey," Voll grinned back. "We were trying to stay under the rainar."

I snorted. "*Rainar*? The human saying is under the *radar*, but good try."

Voll shrugged.

He definitely seemed more confident than before.

"As long as you're not going to proposition my friends, you should come sit by us," I told them, gesturing over my shoulder to the table behind me. "It would be good to chat with some fae."

They exchanged looks again. Trying to decide whether or not to take me up on the offer, I assumed.

"Alright." Ered nodded.

"Cool. Come on." I gestured them over, and they trailed behind me and then took two of the three empty seats at our table. Voll sat to my left, and Ered to his left. Hannah was between me and Elyn, but I didn't mind not being in the middle.

I knew the other two girls were closer to each other than they were to me; that was how three-chick friendships always seemed to go, as far as I'd experienced. But they had different issues with their kings than I did with mine, so it was natural for them to be closer. And I sort of had Auden, which made up for that in a way.

Plus, I was still trying to figure out how to be friends with girls. Which made things a little more challenging, to say the least.

Ered and Voll introduced themselves to Hannah and Elyn, and they admitted that they were my guards—finally.

I didn't know why Auden thought it would be good to keep that a secret, but I was glad it was out in the open.

"So what can you tell us about the fae that the kings might've kept secret?" Hannah asked them.

She studied the men as she ripped a chunk off her roll of the sweet bread the sea fae seemed to eat with everything. I would never complain about that; the bread was too damn good. You could dip it in anything and both would taste even better—but now I'm getting distracted.

Voll and Ered both exchanged uh-oh looks.

"What?" Hannah leaned over the table.

I was curious, but I didn't want to make the ex-soap-makers uncomfortable. They'd been a little shy the last time I'd talked to them, so I wanted to make them feel at ease. Having people be afraid of us wasn't something I wanted.

"We're not really supposed to tell you anything about Avalon," Voll admitted.

Ered elbowed him in the stomach, and the fae let out a quiet, "oof".

"Why not?" Elyn countered.

"Those are conversations you should be having with your husbands," Ered said, shooting Voll a warning.

"Our husbands aren't interested in talking to us," Hannah said. "So, we'll trade you information. Anything you want to know about humans or women is yours, as long as you tell us whatever the kings don't want us to know."

The men exchanged glances again.

Damn their partnership. We needed to get them separate if we were really going to grill them on the sly. Voll was the weak link; he was nice enough and curious enough to break if we got him talking.

"What's a period?" Voll asked.

Ered elbowed him again, and Voll swore under his breath —something about the wist. Whatever the hell that was.

"Once a month, a woman's uterus—this weird organ in here—" Elyn tapped her lower abdomen. "Gets pissed that we're not pregnant and sheds its lining. It hurts like hell, and we bleed out our nether-regions, and get all emotional and cry a lot. But if you feed us enough chocolate, we're fine."

Both men gaped at us.

A glance around the cafeteria-clearing showed me that *all* of the men were gaping at us.

It was kind of nice not to be the one who resembled a fish for once.

"Yeah. You think random boners suck? Try being a woman," Hannah agreed.

"What about sex?" Voll asked. "Does sex hurt?"

Hannah and Elyn looked at me.

Guess it was my turn.

"Sometimes. Depends on the individual girl's anatomy, and how much foreplay is involved. As long as we're enjoying it, we don't mind a little pain usually."

The mood in the cafeteria changed.

Shit.

"Let's change the subject away from sex," Elyn suggested, eyeing the clouds gathering in the sky above us. Kalus was much more friendly and outgoing than his brother, but Merzo seemed to be much more possessive of his wife.

Whether that was a good or bad thing, I didn't know.

"What do women like to do?" Ered asked, shooting Voll a warning glare again.

Hannah shrugged. "Lots of things. We're all different, just like men. Though for the most part, we don't enjoy fighting and killing people."

The "unlike you, with your boredom-wars" part was implied.

"What do *you* like to do?" Ered pointed the question at Hannah, that time.

"I like to help at the dog shelter, and take my dog for walks. And I love to read all kinds of books, and talk about those books with other people who like them. And sometimes, I like to go out with my friends to a bar and drink until I forget the world and feel like a character in one of my favorite books." She shrugged. "I'm pretty simple."

"Love, you are far from simple," Kalus declared, strolling up to our table.

We should've known our little escape wouldn't last long.

Instead of trying to get us to leave, Kalus grabbed the empty chair and plopped it down between me and Hannah. The addition of the chair forced me to scoot a bit so Kalus's big elbows weren't knocking into me, so I gestured for Ered and Voll to scoot over too.

"What are we talking about?" Kalus asked, looking around the table.

"Periods. Sex. Books. The usual," Elyn drawled.

I bit back a snort.

"We're talking about women, then." His lips curved up in a grin and he looked at Hannah. "I'd like to hear more about sex."

"You'd like to hear more about the men I've slept with?" Hannah cooed at him.

His grin vanished.

"Would you like me to tell you about their dicks, too?" she asked. "Or maybe I should list their names, and tell you all about the things they did to me while we were—"

The ground shook.

Elyn coughed something that sounded like, "Cool it."

Maybe she'd learned from taunting her king the day before.

I hoped so; I really didn't want to have to watch someone else die, and then hike across the earth fae's land to wait for him to revive, too.

Kalus's voice was lower, and the ground barely shook at

all when he finally said, "So long as you're imagining my face and body in their place, I'd very much like to hear a recap of your sexual experiences. I'd really enjoy replacing those memories with our own attempts at the positions."

I had to admit, that was a pretty smooth recovery. Especially for an asshole of a virgin fae king.

Hannah looked a bit taken aback by his sudden forwardness, but I'd have guessed that from him. Kalus was clearly the friendliest of the three kings, and friendly people were often harder to intimidate than the quiet ones, because that was just nature.

"What do you think of the rolls?" I asked Hannah and Elyn, changing the subject. "Have you tried dipping them in the potatoes?"

I dunked my roll in potatoes and whatever incredibly delicious gravy-type stuff had been put on my plate, just for emphasis.

"They're pretty good," Elyn said, clearly on board with my subject change. "They kind of remind me of those Hawaiian Sweet Rolls that come in the orange bag," she made a rectangle with her hands, explaining the description of the rolls, I guess.

"Yeah. But less Hawaiian, and more..." I trailed off, not quite sure what words I was looking for.

"Fae?" Elyn's voice was helpful.

"Exactly." I nodded.

"The women help each other when things get uncomfortable," Voll noted. I was pretty sure he meant to whisper that to Ered, but it came out at a normal volume.

"They do." Ered agreed. "They work as a team, but they barely know each other."

Yeah, that was called *necessary teamwork*. If we didn't have each other's backs, we'd be hosed.

"You don't have to know someone to care about them though, do you?" Hannah asked the fae men, her eyes still locked with Kalus's. "Looking out for people is something anyone can do for each other. Something you'd expect two people in an arranged marriage to do. Planning each other's murder, however..." she trailed off.

Clearly, she wanted him to feel like shit.

And I supported that.

CHAPTER 22

"Ah, but there's always more to a relationship than what's obvious, isn't there?" Kalus countered. "What may seem like, oh, a *murder plan*, may actually be something else entirely."

Well, damn.

I actually wanted to see where this conversation was going to go.

"What else could a *murder plan* be?" she demanded.

"I don't know, maybe a plan to return you to your home?" Kalus growled back.

Oh, shit.

That was new.

"What?" Hannah sounded as shocked as I felt. Elyn looked like she was feeling the same thing I was, too.

"We're not in the habit of destroying lives without purpose, Hannah," Kalus's gaze on her was narrowed. "Avalon may not be a place for faeries, but it is a place where strength is celebrated. If you're strong enough to survive getting us back home, I'll be strong enough to ensure that you return home too."

That... was kind of a game-changer.

If we believed him.

From a selfish king's perspective, it did make sense. Life would be easier for the fae if their ex-average-human wives didn't stay in Avalon with them. They could use us, and drop us back on earth. Of course, we wouldn't be treated well with our faery traits, which I was fairly certain would be irreversible. But the fae could ditch us, and come off seeming like the good guys from their perspectives.

Hannah and Elyn did seem to be hoping for an outcome along those lines. They were worried we'd be dragged to Avalon against our will. But personally, I was almost a hundred percent confident that my life on Earth was over.

I didn't know if Auden was on-board with the other kings' plan, but he and the other kings didn't seem to be buddies. And he didn't seem like he was harboring this marry, portal, and ditch plan.

But I could've been wrong about that.

There were a lot of things I could've been wrong about, and I wasn't completely oblivious to that fact.

I just hoped I *wasn't* wrong about most of them.

Voll asked another question about women—luckily, an easy one—and the topic changed to lighter things. I think all of us women were reeling a bit from Kalus's revelation, and trying to figure out how much of it was to be believed and whether or not it was what we wanted.

But we chatted about the differences between men and women until we headed back to the beach house, and it wasn't miserable at all.

Even if our minds were spinning.

HANNAH SHOWERED FIRST, and I cleaned the dishes in the sink that were left over from whatever Auden had made while we were gone. He came out, got irritated with me for doing his dishes, and then disappeared into our room again. Elyn showered while I dried our dishes and put them away, and then it was my turn.

I went into my room to grab clothes, and found Auden laying on the top bunk, reading a book.

I hadn't known he liked to read, so I asked him what book it was. He flashed me the cover, and my lips stretched in a grin. "*Twilight*? By Stephanie Meyer?"

He eyed me. "There were a half a dozen copies of the series at a thrift store we stopped at, so my fae grabbed a few. It's not bad."

"Assuming you like teenage vampires, it's great," I agreed, still grinning as I bent down to grab things out of my bag.

"This Edward guy should've told his woman that he was watching her sleep much earlier than he did," he remarked, as I straightened.

"I think it's supposed to make a point about him being a little awkward, despite how many years he's lived." I shrugged, heading for the door.

Stopping in the doorway, it occurred to me that he seemed to be in a sharing mood again.

"Why doesn't the ocean taste salty to me anymore?" I asked, without turning around.

"You're a sea fae; your skin requires salt to function properly. The salt cleanses you and heals small wounds." He went back to reading, and I got the impression that he wanted me to leave him alone.

"Thanks." I slipped out of the room, and into the bathroom.

The explanation made sense of the way I'd never felt dirty after swimming in the ocean, even when I'd been in the water for hours. I did still have sand in my hair, but that was my own fault for laying in the sand.

I showered quickly and then dressed in some panties and one of my t-shirts—it was still dirty—before heading back to my room.

Auden didn't so much as glance at me as I shut off the light and slipped under the blankets on the bottom bunk, curling up on the bed. I knew he could read just fine even in the dark, thanks to his merman eyes, so I didn't feel bad about crashing.

When I didn't fall asleep right away, I had the urge to open my mouth and ask him to tell me more of his thoughts about *Twilight*.

Assuming the conversation wouldn't be welcomed, I kept my mouth and eyes shut, and instead, went to sleep.

. . .

THE NEXT MORNING was much the same as the one before. Auden woke me up, we ate breakfast, and headed out to the beach. He put the knife in my hand, and our eyes met.

"Four," he said.

"That's too many."

"I don't care."

"Well, you should," I shot back.

"November," he growled.

"Have I ever told you you're an asshole?"

"At least once."

I flipped him the bird, and he reached for my knife hand. Before he could grab it, I cut him.

He nearly fell over with just the one cut.

"Grab my hips, *asshole*." I repeated the insult with emphasis, just to annoy him since he'd told me I said it *at least once*.

He grabbed my hips, though he didn't look thrilled about it.

"I think one's enough," I said, when the cut had healed. Before me and my bloody hand could step back, he wrapped his fingers around mine, around the knife, and lifted it to his chest, slashing it across his pec.

I swore, covering the wound, and he clutched my hips tighter as the knife dropped to the sand. "We're done," I told him, through gritted teeth as that wound healed up too. He was going to be covered in the damned scars, and I'd feel like shit because of it for the rest of who-knew-how-long.

"Grabbed the wisting knife," he ground out.

"No. You need to rest."

He bent over to grab it, and ended up on his *wisting* knees in front of me.

I could've made a really awesome dirty joke, then, but considering my hands were covered in blood and he was kneeling because he was too exhausted to stand, the timing was off and I didn't.

"One more." He put the knife in my hand.

He'd accepted that there wasn't a chance I was doing two more—but apparently still thought he could talk me into a third cut.

"This is ridiculous, Auden."

"I want to go home, November." The words were so pained that I couldn't say no.

With a defeated sigh, I took the knife to his bicep. It would be the last one on the arm, matching the other arm somewhat symmetrically.

"I hate this," I warned him.

His eyes were stony and silvery, colliding with mine as he gripped my hand and helped me cut into his skin.

His eyes glazed over before the cut even healed, and I tried to ease him down to his back on the sand.

Of course, the ocean was having a fit behind us, reacting to my panic as I struggled to control my anger, frustration, fear... whatever I was feeling, it was a mess and I wasn't a fan.

Kalus walked over and crouched beside me, where I lay awkwardly draped halfway over Auden's chest.

"You're going to have to get in the water," he warned.

"I know." I glared at him. "I can walk myself there."

He reached for Auden, and I shoved his hand away. It was my fault the sea king was weak. The least I could do was protect him from the other kings until he could protect himself once again.

"I just want to help you get him to the water," Kalus said, lifting his hands by his head in an overly-human gesture that he meant no harm.

Well... I probably couldn't do that on my own.

"Alright. Don't make me drown you," I warned.

Since he would resurrect, it was a threat I was willing to make.

"Wouldn't dream of it." He flashed me a grin that said he definitely *would* dream of it, as he helped me ease Auden upward.

Without his help, I probably would've resorted to just rolling the big lug down to the water, or trying to convince the ocean to rise high enough to take him for me.

My emotions were still a mess—which the choppy, rising water made clear.

Kalus waded out into the water with me, letting go of Auden when we were deep enough for him to sink without getting a mouthful of sand. The sea king sprouted that gorgeous tail of his, and I turned to the small group of concerned individuals watching us.

"I'll be back when I get this under control," I told the other women. They gave me thumbs-up and grimaces; not very encouraging, but better than nothing.

Submerging myself under the water, I took in a breath of air and welcomed the feeling of my—freaky, I know—gills opening as my scales made an appearance.

I had to admit that the long tail that covered my lower half was beautiful.

Looking out at the water, I told it to take us back to the rocky island I was starting to consider mine.

And, off it dragged us.

Maybe navigating wasn't as hard as I thought.

THE OCEAN TOSSED us back onto the sand not much later. This time, I tried not to faceplant. I failed and still ended up accidentally eating sand, but hey, at least I'd tried.

Rolling myself over, I plopped down to my back on the sand and squinted up at the sun shining brightly above us. Auden was still out on his stomach, and I felt really bad for the guy. Giving me all of his magic was clearly no easy feat.

Closing my eyes to the sun, I basked in the warmth of its rays on my skin as I waited for my merman to wake up.

"NOVEMBER." Auden's hand shook me softly.

"Hmm?" I opened my eyes and looked around blearily, finding myself face-down on the sandy beach I'd been on earlier.

Had I fallen asleep?

I looked at the sky; the sun was setting, so I must've.

But how long had we been on the beach?

"Did you just wake up?" I asked Auden, shocked.

My stomach rumbled loudly, declaring its anger at not being fed.

"Yeah." He scrubbed a hand over his face, his messy blond hair swaying a bit. "We need to get this wisting thing over-with."

That curse again...

"How much power do you have left?"

He glanced out at the ocean, and his forehead wrinkled as his eyes narrowed in focus.

A long minute passed, and then another. I didn't notice anything about the water change, though.

He finally shook his head, looking back at me. "I don't know. Not much."

Well, that wasn't helpful.

"How will we know when you're drained?" I checked.

"I'll reset." He turned his eyes back out to the ocean. "But if I push it too hard before the power's all the way transferred, I'll reset then, too. It'll just cost me a little magic."

Whoa. I didn't know *dying* was the plan for the end the power transfers.

I guess it did make sense, though, given how thoroughly entrenched in the fae their magic was.

Last time we sat on the beach, we'd had a sort of heart-to-heart, but I didn't get the impression that he was anywhere near close to ready to do that again.

"What will happen when I give you your power back in Avalon?" I asked.

"Hopefully, you develop magic of your own. Nonmagical beings can't survive long in Avalon."

I frowned. "Why not?"

"It's hard to explain. In the simplest terms, the magic acts as a parasite or disease that eats at anyone without magic to protect them."

Yikes.

"What if I don't develop magic?"

"Then I'll bring you back here, and we'll come up with another solution."

Something told me that the other solution would be to ditch me with the humans, leaving me completely at their mercy. Who knew if I would even resurrect like the other fae if they killed me—or what I'd be, exactly.

"You'll leave me," I said flatly.

"If there's no way for you to survive in Avalon." He stared out at the ocean. "Your world is hideous. The colors are dull, and the world has so little life that it looks to my magic for guidance on how to act."

"With that attitude, you probably think humans are hideous too, with our dull-colored hair and eyes compared to you fae bastards."

"Humans are hideous, yes."

"Asshole."

"You're not a human. It wasn't an insult to you; becoming a faery suits you well."

"I felt pretty as a human at least some of the time. Now, I feel like an alien."

Or a mermaid, I guess. Though fish-women did kind of sound like aliens, when I thought about it.

He muttered something incomprehensible. I didn't want to know what.

We sat there until he was in good enough shape to swim back, barely talking at all, and then headed home.

CHAPTER 23

AUDEN WENT to bed when we got back to the beach house. He'd looked like crap though, so I threw together a bowl of mashed potatoes, corn, and shredded chicken. It was the only thing I'd ever actually *seen* him eat, despite all the times he'd cooked for me and then vanished. I didn't want him not to like what I made, so I stuck with the safe option.

I took the bowl in and found him almost asleep already. He barely opened his eyes when I walked over, but opened them wider when he saw that I was holding food.

"You should eat before you go to sleep."

His eyes narrowed, and he scanned me as if he was looking for proof that I'd poisoned the food or was trying to mock him or something.

I waited far too long for him to take the food, and then rolled my eyes.

"Fine. Don't." I started to turn away, with the food, but he grabbed the bowl before I could.

My eyes turned back to him, and I watched him sniff the bowl.

"Seriously? Where would I get poison?" I shot back.

"There are many fae who wish me dead."

"I'm the only faery who does, though," I muttered, shaking my head and turning away.

"Thank you," he said, as I left the room.

The words were so shocking I stopped in my tracks and opened my mouth to ask him if he was on drugs.

I heard a sharp inhale before I could ask, and then a muttered curse.

"It hurts even from this close?" I asked him, turning back around to look at him.

His jaw was clenched, and he didn't answer.

"Seriously?" I gave him an exasperated look.

He gave me a dark one back. "I'm not a damned invalid, November."

I crossed the room, heading back over to him. "How many times do I have to tell you to call me Noa?"

"November fits you better."

"I think I should get to choose which name fits me best," I shot back.

"No one chooses their own name."

"Plenty of people choose their own *nicknames* though."

"You're a queen, November. Noa is hardly a name fitting of the first queen of Avalon in centuries."

"You're the one who mocked my name the first day I got here," I said, exasperated.

He didn't respond.

Maybe he regretted that.

Or maybe he was just trying to annoy me; with him, it was hard to say.

I folded myself into the bottom bunk and stared up at the rock slab holding up the massive man above me. I waited for eating sounds, and didn't hear anything.

Auden didn't strike me as a man who would swallow his pride to thank me for something he didn't intend to eat, which meant something was wrong.

And the only reason I could come up with for him not eating?

The bond.

"Does it still hurt while I'm this close to you?"

Silence.

That would be a yes.

"How bad is the pain?"

No response.

With an inward sigh, I slipped off the bed and stood, climbing up onto the ledge of the rock holding my mattress so I could look at Auden face to face. "Tell me."

His expression was stony.

"I don't give a shit about your fae secrety-traditions, Chaos. Tell me the damn truth or I'll throw you in the ocean this time."

Instead of hardening, his expression seemed to grow a bit softer as the corner of his lips tilted slightly. It was the first tiny, minuscule hint of a smile that I'd ever seen from him, and it was freakin' gorgeous.

"It's constant unless we're touching. But it doesn't get terrible until you're about a room away."

My eyebrows shot upward. "How long has it been like this?"

"It's a new development."

Meaning, since those last few transfers?

The only time I'd touched him was when I was bleeding him, and when we'd been swimming together—or being pushed around by the ocean together, I guess.

Stepping off the bed frame, I walked around to the ladder and climbed up it. Balancing off the edge, I swept my hand toward Auden in a shooing motion. "Scoot up."

"To where?" He shot me a look that said I clearly didn't realize how monstrously large he was, even in the king sized bed.

"Just fold your legs a bit."

He pulled them to the side a little—not much, but enough for me to squeeze in.

"If all we need is physical contact, your foot against my leg should be plenty while you get some rest. We've got to be close to the end of this, right?"

"I wisting hope so," he muttered.

It couldn't have been easy to be an all-powerful king who couldn't even manage to keep himself upright anymore.

Grabbing his ankle, I dragged his foot over so his toes touched the outside of my knee. "Eat your food and take a nap. I'll protect you."

He snorted, and my lips twitched upward toward a grin.

He cleared the bowl, then handed me the book sitting up beside one of his pillows when he noticed me eyeing it.

"When I wake up, we'll do that last transfer or two," he warned, handing me the empty bowl when I reached for it.

"Sure." I was ready for this to be over too. Or at least, to see what came next. Since my future as a pianist was dead, I might as well go see a new world and figure out what it was like to be a faery in Avalon, right?

He got comfortable, and I couldn't help but study him as his body relaxed. It was the first time I'd ever really seen him that way; even on the couch that one night, he'd looked uncomfortable. I guess having his magic touching him was what he needed to feel and sleep well again.

I read while he slept, and over the next few hours, he slowly slid further down the bed until his legs were draped over my lap, folded up a bit so they were resting on me from the mid-thigh and down. I didn't want to wake him up just to make him scoot away, so I kept glancing down at getting an eyeful of buff thigh that did annoying things to my lower belly.

I refused to be attracted to my husband, though, regardless of how attractive he was. I couldn't be interested in a guy who was constantly angry, even if he was just having a bad month. Maybe his perspective would change a bit when we were back in Avalon, but I wasn't going to let myself fall for someone who would only piss me off.

I respected myself too much to settle for that kind of relationship.

· · ·

MY STOMACH STARTED to rumble after a few hours, and I heaved a sigh as I started to feel like my body was going to start eating itself. I didn't want to get up—Auden was clearly in bad shape if he was still sleeping soundly this much later. But I also wanted food.

The door opened a crack halfway through the afternoon, and Hannah peeked inside. "Are you hungry?" she whispered.

"Yes." I tried to scoot closer to her, but Auden's legs were too heavy.

"We brought food," Hannah said, slipping inside. She eyed the silently-sleeping Auden, and then eyed me.

"The bond is strong enough now that it hurts him if we're not touching," I whispered to her. "He couldn't even eat."

Her eyebrows shot upward. "Wow."

"Yeah." I accepted the high-piled plate, my mouth officially watering. "Thank you so much."

"It's the least we can do since you took the king-bullet." She winked.

I guess I had saved them from some more issues with their kings by agreeing to be the one who opened the portal.

She slipped out of the room, and I started in on the food tower.

It was only a minute after the door closed when Auden moved a bit.

He sniffed the air, and I would've grinned if I wasn't busy stuffing my face.

"You have food?" he asked, his voice rough with sleep. He still didn't open his eyes, or sit up, or even move his legs off my lap.

"Yup." I kept eating.

He finally opened his eyes halfway, watching me eat for a minute before his gaze dipped to my lap—and his legs, covering it. "Sorry," he mumbled, lifting them off of me and turning so he was sitting upright.

"It's probably fair for you to use me as a footrest, since I'm holding most of your magic," I told him, as he turned so his back faced the wall, the same way mine did.

We sat shoulder-to-shoulder, but our skin didn't touch. While my legs fit on the bed just fine because they weren't all that long, his hung over the railing by a lot.

"I'm not shy about my body; you don't have to be afraid to touch your shoulder to mine," I told him. "We're stuck in this hot mess of a marriage together; if touching gives you some relief from that pain, we might as well do it."

He scooted a half an inch closer, moving just enough so our shoulders met through our clothes. I didn't know if that would give him relief, but I doubted he'd tell me either way, so I didn't ask.

We sat in silence for a few minutes, while I kept eating. I was slowing down, though, and Auden kept glancing over at me and my food.

"You hungry?" I asked him, setting the fork down on the half-full plate and handing it over to him.

He eyed the food, not accepting it right away. "That's yours."

"I'm done." I set it down on his lap, since he was refusing it. "I'm sure it takes a lot of food to power all this." I wiggled my finger around toward him.

"On Earth, it does," he agreed. "Not on Avalon, though."

I lifted an eyebrow toward him as he took a bite of the food I'd left him.

"You have to trade me information," he said, as he swallowed his food.

I rolled my eyes. "Seriously? This again?"

"It's a method of preventing one person from having more power than another in any given friendship or relationship."

Well, that wasn't so crazy.

"I worked as a waitress before everything happened with you guys coming to Earth and whatnot," I explained. "At a breakfast food place. They'd been trying to talk me into accepting a promotion and becoming a manager for the past year, but I was afraid if I took it, it would be like accepting that I would never become a pianist."

"And that's what you wanted to do with your life, then? Be a pianist?"

"Yes. Playing the piano makes me feel alive," I admitted.

"We don't have an instrument like that in Avalon. I'd never heard anyone play it before you," he remarked. "You're good."

"Thanks." I fiddled with a piece of my hair. Since it was so freakin' long, it was good for awkward moments, at least.

"The ocean provides us with the majority of our sustenance in Avalon," he explained. "It's the same for the other types of fae and their natural gifts, as well. Most fae only eat two light meals a day, so it's been strange to be hungry all the time on earth."

"Ugh. That sounds awful. I hate being hungry." I tilted my head back against the wall. "Let's be friends."

There was a pause.

"Sorry, that came out kind of abruptly. It's just... we're *unbreakable companions* now, right? Even if we get this stuff with the magic and the different worlds figured out, we're still married. Permanently. And if we're going to be stuck together for the rest of our unforeseeably-long lives, we could at least be friends."

He still didn't respond immediately, but he didn't look pissed this time, at least.

"I'm also willing to promise not to sleep with any other guys, so I don't disgrace you or whatever. As long as you're willing to agree to the same—though there aren't really any other faeries to hit on. Other than my friends."

He gave me a sideways glance. "You've only just become a faery."

"I told you about my family situation; I'm not going to change my mind. Cheating isn't something I condone, in any way. If we're stuck together, I'm going to be loyal. Period."

There was a tense moment before he finally nodded. "We can attempt a friendship."

Well, it wasn't the answer I was hoping for, but it was better than a straight-up "no".

"Thanks, I think."

He shot me a look I couldn't read. "Friendship is not entered into lightly in Avalon. Most fae have only a few people that they trust."

I guessed I could see that. The fae seemed to stick with a chosen one or two people for the most part. Though, Auden didn't seem to hang around with much of *anyone*.

"Where are your friends?"

"Back in Avalon." He didn't seem like he was going to add to that in any way, and I didn't want to push him, so I kept my mouth shut. "Where are yours?"

"Other than Hannah and Elyn, I don't really have any close friends," I admitted.

I felt kind of stupid for admitting it, though. I'd never collected friends the way a lot of people seemed to, and I'd rather spend my time alone with my piano than with someone I didn't really want to be hanging out with. That made me a bit of a loner, but most of the time, I preferred it that way. I did have a group of guy friends that I got together with sometimes before the world started to end, but they all had their own lives, so we sort of drifted apart.

"You only just met them," he countered.

"I know."

He was silent, eating quietly. Probably feeling pity for me or something, since he seemed to have friends of his own that he liked enough not to care whether or not he and I became friends too.

When he was done eating, he slid off the bed in one

smooth movement and landed on his feet. "Let's get this over with."

When he strode out of the room, something lodged in my throat a bit.

It was time to get the fae back to Avalon.

And me, with them.

CHAPTER 24

THE OTHER KINGS AND QUEENS, along with Ien, Ered, and Voll, gathered on the beach with us.

"We'll start the portal while you're reviving," Ien explained to Auden.

"No. The portal will require November's blood to stay open long enough to fit everyone through, and I don't trust any of you to be careful enough with her," Auden growled. "You wait for me to come back before opening it."

Ah, yes. The dreaded reforming.

I wasn't looking forward to being left alone with these other fae. Not at all.

"Very well." Ien bobbed his head, his expression remaining the same cheerful-neutral he seemed to have perfected. It occurred to me, in the moment, that I didn't know anything about who he was or who he had been before he came to Earth. That hadn't seemed like an important piece of information... until we were talking about going back there.

I didn't really know who Merzo and Kalus had been before the portal, either. And that didn't sit well with me—not at all. Even Auden was a bit of a mystery, though I knew slightly more about him than the others.

"Maybe we should wait until tomorrow," I suggested. I'd finally gotten Auden talking to me like I was a person; maybe with another day, I could get more information from him.

"No. We do this today," Merzo said sharply.

Auden took a step toward the guy, and I eyed him.

What was he doing?

Merzo quickly lifted his hands. "I mean no disrespect. I'm just ready to get back to Avalon, like the rest of us."

There was a long pause before Auden finally turned to me, knife in his hand.

"Last time," he told me, his gaze steady. "Don't stop until I'm gone."

My mouth opened, and then closed as I swallowed hard. "Are you sure?"

I really, really hated the idea of that.

And how would we even know if he'd died because his magic was empty or because he'd pushed too hard, too fast?

"Positive." He put the knife in my hand. I usually avoided looking at it, because I felt terrible about using it to cut Auden, but this time I glanced down at it. The color was a shimmery silver that reminded me of his eyes, and of our skin when swimming.

He frowned, looking at me like I was doing something

wrong. "Don't be afraid. A few cuts, and I'll be out of your hair for a few hours."

I scoffed. "Have you seen my hair? If I had you tangled up in it, you'd never get out."

His lips curved upward, and I got it—that smile.

The first one I'd ever seen on him.

And it was even more gorgeous than I expected.

It didn't last, though.

He hauled me over to the water, setting me on my feet when we were deep enough that it reached my hips.

"Don't let them touch you," he growled at me.

And then he took my hand, using me to cut into him. One slice slid across his chest—and then another, and another. All three were close enough together that my hands could cover them, but too fast for me to stop him.

"Come on," I hissed at him, pressing my hands to his chest even while my eyes were locked with his.

I watched him slowly grow more out of it as the last of his magic flooded into me. It felt like I was drowning in the magic—like I could barely breathe as it filled my abdomen and pumped through my veins.

The cuts closed up... and then Auden vanished.

I stumbled backward, staring at my hands as sharp pain tore through my chest, so fierce and hot that a scream cut through my throat.

Someone's hands wrapped around my arms, and then they dragged me up to the beach. My vision cleared even though pain throbbed in my chest so sharply that tears dripped down my face.

I crashed to my knees on the sand, clutching my chest as Ien stalked toward me with a knife. The ocean churned behind me, the water rising by the second.

"Hurry," Kalus growled at Ien.

A massive group of fae descended from the sky; so many more than I could count.

Ien grabbed my hair, slashing a few inches off one end before he sliced his knife through my shoulder.

A cry escaped me as blood poured down my arm. I tried to shove at him, tried to move my arms, but there was some kind of pressure forcing me on my knees. Air—it had to be some kind of air from the sky fae.

Ien shoved the hair into the wound, soaking my lost strands in my blood, and I cried out again.

The ocean crashed at my feet behind me, rushing up past my knees and over the feet of the gathering fae. I still didn't know how to control it—I still didn't know how to make it do what I wanted. Not even to protect myself.

"Hurry," Kalus snarled again, ripping the bloody knife out of Ien's hand and tossing it into the ocean. "Who knows how fast that bastard will revive without any magic tied to him."

Auden?

Were they talking about Auden?

I hoped so.

Ien crushed the bloody hair in his hand and shouted a few words in the fae language that I hadn't heard before. There was no translation for them as far as I could tell, unless that gift had temporarily left the world with Auden.

A massive portal, twice the size of the beach house, bloomed to life in front of me, sucking away my energy with it. I would've crashed to my hands and knees if the air hadn't been holding me in place.

The one I'd seen on the videos of the fae's arrival was red and glowing; this one was a sea-foam green, and radiated light. It had a massive, round, rippling surface that reminded me of a calm ocean, and was partially transparent, as if it was only sort-of there. It throbbed with life, and somehow, felt like a part of me.

Through the portal, my eyes landed on Hannah and Elyn, who were kicking and fighting their kings as Merzo and Kalus dragged the ex-average-humans through the door to Avalon. Another fae followed them, carrying Hannah's dog. They stepped inside the rippling light and vanished, and the air holding me down immediately let up.

"Grab the queen," Ien called out to another group of fae charging toward the shimmering portal on the beach.

Voll and Ered changed directions, coming for me.

Crap.

Hannah and Elyn needed help, but Auden was still in some kind of between-world.

And if I was the only one who could make a portal back to Avalon, then I had to stay on Earth until Auden could go back too.

My mind was foggy with the pain throbbing in my chest, but I was focused enough to know what I needed to do—that I needed to figure out a way to stay until Auden was revived.

The ocean had responded to my thoughts before, so I urged it to come up and sweep me away.

It swept up toward me, but not strong enough to pull me into the ocean.

A shout went up from the faeries as the water rose, though, and Ien charged for the portal.

Ered grabbed me by the arm, and I mentally yelled at the water as I fought the fae dragging me through the sand.

A shadow rose, and I turned my head to see a massive wave gathering in the ocean just off the beach. I wasn't positive it was a tsunami, but it was at least four or five times the height of my apartment building.

And shit, that wasn't what I had wanted.

Shouts and frantic yells rose up from the fae as they poured into the portal. I felt the magic holding it up wavering, somewhere within me.

Ered dropped his grip on my arm, taking off toward the portal. I couldn't imagine he was afraid of the water, being a sea fae and whatnot, so I had to assume he was just worried about the gate to Avalon closing without him inside it.

He dove through right behind the last of the other fae, barely clearing it before the tidal wave crashed down on Avalon Island.

The water engulfed me, slamming me hard into the ground. The portal vanished in front of my eyes before the ocean whisked me away.

I knew I needed to calm down to smooth out the ocean, but between the chest pain and everything else that had just happened seemingly out of nowhere, I couldn't manage to focus on anything.

The ocean tossed me like a ragdoll, much harder than ever before. I was completely at its mercy, and the pain in my chest never lessened.

After a while, I was so dizzy and out of it that I couldn't handle it anymore. I silently urged the ocean to take me back to that little island it had dropped me on the last few times I lost control.

Sure enough, the water spat me out on the shore of that barren little rock shortly after.

Choppy waves battled higher than the island around me, but left the entirety of that small island dry. It was doing what I wanted, the same way it had on the beach. I just didn't know exactly how to make sure that happened... or how to control it.

"It would be cool if you could calm down, now," I told the ocean, trying to get it to shrink back down.

Without being in the human part of the world, I had no way of knowing whether or not my reaction was already causing more of the same terrible destruction that the fae had caused when they first arrived. But I really, really hoped it wouldn't.

And I didn't really want to know if it was, because I was already doing everything I could to stop it.

The ocean didn't calm, and the water didn't lower.

I needed music to calm me, but with the throbbing pain in my chest, I wasn't sure even my favorite songs would fix anything.

I'd hit the sea castle with a tidal wave, so the chances of the island coming out untouched may as well have been nothing.

The sea castle was gone, but the fae were safe—or at least back home in Avalon, if not safe. Which meant I didn't need to worry about them, yet.

Hannah and Elyn were... probably in deep shit. They would definitely need help.

I paced the small beach on my island, digging the butt of my palm into the center of my chest in an attempt to shrink the fiery pain there.

"One thing at a time, Noa," I muttered to myself. "One problem first."

And the main problem?

Auden.

Or rather, the lack of Auden.

Since I had all of his magic, he'd be in terrible pain when he resurrected if I wasn't anywhere near him.

And the other fae had been worried he'd revive quickly. If their worry was correct, we were in trouble.

But if it wasn't, then theoretically, I still had a few hours before he came back. Finding the plate at the center of Avalon Island might be challenging considering I was lost in the ocean somewhere, but I had time to figure that out too.

A few hours wasn't a lot of time, but it could be enough.

I'd get back to Avalon Island and find Auden. Then, I'd worry about figuring out how to open a portal. Hopefully, Auden would know the magic words.

He would help me get us to Avalon, and then we could

worry about finding the other two queens. I'd be useless in fae-land without Auden anyway; it wasn't like I knew my way around, or understood how to use the sea magic, or anything, really. In my heart, I was still the average human girl I'd been when the government sacrificed me to the fae.

And maybe I was average, but average didn't translate to helpless.

"Okay, ocean," I told it, though it didn't seem to give a crap as to what I had to say. "I need to go back to Avalon Island."

The ocean continued its choppy movements, moving rapidly as it towered a few feet above my head. It was still staying off the island, though, by some miracle.

I hadn't had any success telling it what to do, but... maybe it just wanted me to show it, or feel it, in my mind. That was the only way I'd controlled it in the past, so that made the most sense.

With a muttered, "Please don't kill me," I threw myself into the waves.

The ocean whisked me away, and I focused my mind on Avalon Island, silently urging the water to carry me there even as I was thrown about by the current.

I was at its mercy, not understanding the way it moved well enough to turn myself and let it guide me instead of just carrying me. But getting a ride was much better than getting stuck on that island in the middle of nowhere forever, especially while my friends needed me.

And strangely enough, that umbrella of *friends* had come to include Auden.

The jerk of a sea king who had chosen me last, had become someone I cared about enough to stay on Earth instead of letting the rest of the fae whisk me through their portal where I could help the other ex-average-humans.

Our friendship was definitely still tentative, but I liked to think we were something of a team. And even if he didn't agree, he'd told me things I needed to know and protected me. And after I dragged him back to Avalon with me, I would officially have done the same for him. So even if he still didn't agree to call me his friend, he could at least consider me his partner.

I hoped our partnership wouldn't end the moment his feet touched down in Avalon's soil or dirt or water, but I wasn't oblivious. I knew that there was a decent chance that he'd turn on me the way the other kings had turned on Hannah and Elyn. But going in with my eyes open didn't hurt anything; it just made me more prepared.

I'd learn as much as I could about Avalon before Auden got back to those real friends of his and went back to heatedly ignoring me, and I'd figure out a way to save the other girls.

After all, if we average humans didn't have each other's backs, who would?

CHAPTER 25

EVERYTHING WAS GOING fine with the ocean, until it slammed me into a tree.

The massive trunk had come out of seemingly nowhere, but I collided with it so hard that it ripped the breath out of me and I saw stars.

I wheezed in the water, sucking in liquid as I struggled to catch my breath. At least, as well as a person could catch their breath while breathing water.

Swimming up toward the surface, my head broke the water. I looked around to see how the hell a tree that big had ended up in the middle of the ocean, and noticed that the water seemed to have calmed a bit. Now that I wasn't beneath the waves, the current had slowed dramatically and now was weak enough that I could ignore it.

My eyes widened as I realized that the ocean was still at least five or six feet higher than it should've been. Maybe even more. I could see the top of the gazebo we'd "gotten married" in a few feet off to my left, and found branches and leaves that were part of the massive forest stretched out in front of me. I couldn't see the ground anymore though, which was a problem because I didn't know how to find the island's center with the damn thing under water.

My emotions were still too wild to calm myself to the point of the water lowering back to where it was supposed to be, so I dove down a bit and swam over to the gazebo.

My eyes caught on the path. It was only visible because of its indentation in the dirt road, but it was there.

Rather than walking it, I swam it.

My hair spread out behind me, my belly nearly grazing the path stretched out beneath me.

It was eerie, underwater. Seeing fish swimming through the bushes, watching them weave around tree trunks as I passed them... it definitely gave me the goosebumps. But my head pounded along with my heart by then, both pushing me forward, toward Auden.

The water seemed to have stilled, the currents calm now that my mind was focused and quieting.

The other fae hadn't known how long it would take Auden to resurrect; they'd been worried it would be fast because he was basically human. But it had taken Merzo a long time because of his missing magic; I would've assumed that meant it would take Auden even longer.

So I continued onward.

I could've swam faster if I pushed the water to work with me, but I was afraid of whatever effect it would have on the trees and wildlife I'd already submerged. I hoped I hadn't killed too many things, and guilt crept into my chest, making my heart work even harder than it already was working.

The abandoned earth castle was even creepier than the forest while it was underwater. My eyes traced the outside of the brown stone building as I swam around it, sticking to the path I'd been following. My mind struggled to put the outside of the spooky stone fortress together with the simple soil-smelling building that I'd been in so many times with Hannah and Kalus.

A shiver slid down my spine as I left the castle behind me, and it had nothing to do with the temperature of the water.

I followed the path for a while longer before I found that large ceramic disk that reminded me of a big plate. Breaking the surface, I looked around for evidence that Auden had beaten me there. My chest still hurt like crazy, so I doubted he had, but I checked anyway.

Seeing nothing that made me think he was back yet, I submerged myself in the water again and swam back to the plate. I didn't want to miss him, so I let myself sink to the bottom of the water and draped my tailed-self out on the ground like it was any other day and I was just napping on the island-turned-ocean-floor for fun.

The dirt and rocks dug uncomfortably into my scales and skin, but I ignored them. With the adrenaline that had followed the portal's appearance all but gone, I was starting to feel tired.

Really, really tired.

I wouldn't let myself sleep, but every part of my body

grew heavy with exhaustion, and it took everything I had just to keep myself awake.

I don't know how long I stayed there, watching that plate, before Auden appeared on it in a flash of light.

His chest rose as he took a breath, and his eyes flew open as he jerked upright. The water level had gone down a little, so his head cleared the surface when he stood up straight.

He'd taken a breath, so where was his tail?

I swam up, utterly exhausted as I scanned him for injuries. He was coughing up water, his body looking weak. He stumbled, and I grabbed his arms to hold him upright.

My tail shifted back to legs, and I sank downward as the water engulfed my head.

Crap. I was too short.

Auden tugged me upward, and I treaded water with my legs as I shoved my fingers to his neck, looking for his pulse.

"You're alive?" I demanded.

"I'm fine." His eyes lingered on me longer than they should've, and then finally, he dragged his gaze off me and looked around the clearing. "Where are the others?"

"Gone."

He blinked.

"They attacked me as soon as you disappeared. The portal opened, and they tried to drag me through it, but I sort of... drowned the island."

Auden snarled. "Where did they cut you?"

"Here." I tapped my shoulder, though my hair was practically glued to it. "I'm fine, though. It doesn't hurt or anything. I think I heal as fast you now that—what are you doing?"

His fingers were peeling hair off my skin, trying to expose my shoulder to the air.

He stopped when my shoulder was bare, and a string of fae curses spewed from his lips. The only one I recognized was *wist* in a few of its different forms, and I still had yet to learn the definition of that one.

I tilted my head awkwardly, trying to see what he was looking at.

My stomach turned to stone when I saw neon-purple veins around the healed scar on my skin. "What is that?"

"*Ovapeldo*," he said, the word gravelly. It didn't translate automatically, so I had no idea what that meant. "A magical infection."

Well that didn't sound good.

"This is why I told them to wait. *Wisting* kings," he swore.

His thumb brushed over it, and he snarled again as the purple color grew pinker for a moment before reverting back to the bright purple. It was a beastly sound; he was really, really pissed.

"What does it mean?"

"Magic must be freely given, or its use taints the users and the owner. Every one of the fae who took advantage of your magic will owe you now; the *ovapeldo* connects them back to you."

"What do they owe me?" I frowned. I'd heard stories

about faery bargains when I was a kid; that was one of the things they were supposedly known for.

"It's not..." He shoved a hand through his hair, looking frazzled.

I'd never seen Auden frazzled before. Mostly, I'd only seen anger from him, though it seemed like we were getting to a few more honest emotions.

"It doesn't hurt you. Or at least it won't, not yet. They don't necessarily owe you something, but their magic is now yours until they've done something to make amends for the thievery."

"Well, that doesn't sound so bad. The fae who went through the portal are powerless now?"

"Yes and no. Their power is still theirs; they just have to kill you or help you to get it back."

Oh.

Yikes.

"Why did they leave you?" He studied me, the water still around our shoulders as we stood on the ceramic disc.

Well, as *he* stood on the ceramic disc and I treaded water, holding on to his shoulder with one of my hands so he wasn't in pain.

He continued, "I'd assume they were planning to kill you to free themselves of the debt as soon as they got back to Avalon."

"They wanted to take me with them, but the wave I sort of created wiped out the portal. They barely got through in time." I shrugged. "I'll just revive if I die, right? So we should let them kill me, and everything will be fine."

"No. Faeries are immortal, but killable. You don't revive."

My mouth opened, and then closed, and then opened again a moment later when my mind was done spinning.

Fish-mouth again, I know.

"So they were going to permanently kill me to get their magic back?" I checked.

"And leave me here, so that the sea kingdom would end with me," he growled.

I didn't know why that would be the end of the sea kingdom, but nodded.

"So you're not friends with any of those guys, right?"

He scowled. "I told you, all of my friends are back in Avalon. Most are wind fae." Auden's eyes turned to the mountains at our backs, his eyes scanning the towering peaks. "We need to get to dry land so I can see how far the *ovapeldo* extends."

"Why?" I asked, though I swam beside him as he let go of me and headed toward the mountains. He was much slower than usual; he had to be feeling the absence of his magic. We needed to figure out a way to get it back to him, though that would have to wait until we were in Avalon.

"As it spreads, the other men's magic will begin to permanently seep into yours—or mine, I suppose. Ours. I'm not sure where the cutoff is at this point." The words were absentminded as his gaze scanned the rocky cliffs ahead of us. He was trying to figure out where to climb out of the water; I could tell.

"So?"

"*So* just possessing one fae's magic that way for more than a few weeks would infect ours, and you hold the power of over a thousand fae. Bits of their magic will seep into ours, rendering it unstable. And when a magic as strong as mine is unstable..." he trailed off.

I got the feeling the outcome looked something like Earth

Devastation and loss, everywhere.

"I'll give your magic back as soon as we're back in Avalon, so we don't have to deal with that. Unless the magic itself is infected?"

"No. The infection is in your skin, so it's nontransferable. But the impact of the infection on your system would be far greater without any magic to cushion it, so that's not an option."

He led me to a rocky part of the mountain. My bare foot caught on a sharp rock, and I swore as it sliced through my skin. Auden grabbed me in his arms, hauling me out of the water. He climbed up the mountain a few feet before sitting down and plopping me on the rock beside him, and then grabbed my foot and inspected it. "It'll be healed in a few seconds," he said, setting my foot back down.

I watched him, a bit in shock as he gathered all my hair in his gigantic fist, twisting it and lifting it up off my neck. He studied my shoulder, moving my arm as he clinically looked over every inch of the skin exposed on my back. I felt a bit warm with his eyes on me like that, but I knew he wasn't checking me over for anything but the infection.

When his fingers brushed over my lower back, I nearly jumped out of my skin.

He muttered an apology, dropping my hair so all eight-hundred pounds of it brushed the ground and stuck to my back.

"Legs down," he warned, his attention moving to my front.

My legs flattened out in front of me, and my eyes shot skyward as he looked over my skin, his face way too close to some parts of my body.

"Lay down," he instructed, his gaze clinical.

With an accusatory-stare, I lowered myself to my back and peered up at him. He studied my hip much longer than he'd studied any other part of me. He even started to reach for it, but thought better and pulled his hand back. "Alright." He offered me the hand he'd nearly touched me with, and helped me to a sitting position.

"We have a few weeks," he told me. "But we need to get back to Avalon, so I can start slaughtering people."

CHAPTER 26

I BLINKED AT HIM.

"Slaughtering people?"

"That's the easiest way to free you from the infection. The fae will revive, though their power will be much less when they return." His voice was even, as if he didn't have a problem with the idea of a massacre.

Although, was it really a massacre if they came back to life?

I was leaning toward no.

"Merzo and Kalus took Hannah and Elyn," I changed the subject.

"The bond wouldn't give them another option."

"I'm still confused by your relationship with them. Are you friends? Enemies? Neighbors?"

"Not friends or enemies, but something between the two. They expect me to fall as fast as the previous sea kings have, while their kingdoms have been allies for centuries as the brothers ruled in tandem. They assume that because I'm new to the leadership game, they can shape me. Or at least, they used to assume that. I've proved them wrong in the last few weeks, I'm sure."

"Aren't you?" I checked. "New to the game."

He didn't answer right away, so I waited.

"Yes and no," he finally admitted. "I've been right-hand to the wind king for centuries, leading his armies."

"There are wind fae and sky fae? How are they different?"

"Many of their gifts are similar, but the difference is in where their power comes from. The wind fae gather strength in the blowing gales; the sky fae's power originates in the clouds, storms, and sky above the ground, though gravity forces them to live on the land like the rest of us. The wind fae are the fourth-largest power, but we—they—have no desires of more land or power. They don't fight in wars unless someone directly attacks them, and when they fight, they win."

Ah. Well, I couldn't say that didn't sound good. The whole going-to-war-out-of-boredom thing had seemed pretty screwed up to me since the beginning.

"Alright. Is it time?" I asked him, making my way to my feet. We'd both needed a bit of a break, and I *really* needed some food and sleep, but putting the portal off any longer wasn't going to help anything.

"Yup."

Something about the response made him seem human in a way that I found myself liking tremendously. "Are you going to chop off my hair too?" I looked for the chunk of hair that had been cut, but it all seemed to be the same length once again. Guess it had already grown back.

He scowled. "No. Hair is a weak alternative to a faery herself. You'll be opening the portal."

My eyebrows lifted skyward. "You sure about that?"

"Yes."

No other explanation. Just a simple *yes*.

Well, I guess it was nice to have someone believe in me. Even if that belief was probably misplaced.

"Alright. How do I do it?"

"Avalon has become a part of you, through my magic. Though you've never been there, you'll need to lock on to a mental image or feeling of a particular location. It doesn't matter where you take us—we'll be fine anywhere because we're sea fae. But once you've locked on to a place, you'll need to say a few words with the blood of Avalon on your fingers."

Okay, yeah, he was majorly overestimating my abilities and my connection to his home.

"The blood of Avalon?"

"Faeries carry Avalon's blood, fae carry Earth's."

Um, what?

I didn't even have to ask about that; he could tell that I was about to and answered before I could.

"The connection between our worlds is ancient. The only world we can portal to and from is this one. Legends say that faeries alone were Avalon's first residents, and that the fae are simply humans who gained faery magic through coming to Avalon with the seductive, vibrant faery woman. Supposedly, it's the reason for the differences in our ears." Auden gestured to his ears—curved, like a human's.

Huh.

"Well, you're just an infinite source of information now, aren't you?"

He flashed me a dark look. "You could've abandoned me here and gone with the other fae, so in staying, you saved my life. I owe you."

"Well, I guess that's good enough reasoning." I wouldn't point out that the other fae would've killed me the moment I crossed over to Avalon now that I'd become a holding-place for their magic.

"Your skin will heal quickly, so first we'll start by finding that mental picture of Avalon." He dragged me back to the portal instructions.

"Alright, what does it look like?"

"Like earth, but cleaner and with more contrast. The brights are brighter, the darks are darker, and it smells like...home."

"Smells like home? Seriously?" I gave him an exasperated look.

The corner of his lips lifted, just slightly, in an almost-smile. "Close your eyes."

I rolled them, first, but then closed them.

His chest gently met my back. I stiffened a bit as his arms went around the outsides of mine, engulfing me.

"I'm not flirting with you," he told me, the murmured

words enough to give me goosebumps and make me jump at the same time. "I'm helping."

Ah.

Right.

Great.

"Helping a lot, clearly," I drawled, hoping he didn't notice my goosebumps or the way I was trying hard not to melt into the comfortable strength of the muscles surrounding me.

"Shush." The soft word surprised me, coming from the gigantic, typically-angry fae behind me. "Because we're *kompells*, physical contact should bring up feelings of home, which should remind our magic of Avalon."

"*Kompells?*"

"Unbreakable companions. It's another form of *kompelenos.*"

I could definitely get used to Auden actually telling me things. It was a thousand times better than being in the dark, or trying to barter for information I needed to know.

"Okay, but—"

"Shh. Keep your eyes closed, and try to think of home."

I was about a thousand percent sure this plan wasn't going to work, but I shut my mouth and kept my eyes closed.

After a minute of silence, I started to feel it—that homey feeling he'd told me about. It wasn't coming from Avalon, though. It was coming from him.

It was a feeling of safety, security, protection. Maybe peace, too. The feeling that I could be whoever I wanted to be, and would be loved for whoever I was.

And shit, it about brought tears to my eyes.

I didn't just feel at home... I felt *loved* in Auden's arms.

Which was absolutely a terrible way to feel, because he was always angry and we barely knew each other. That emotion wasn't love—it was magic. The same magic that turned me into a mermaid and made the ocean respond to my emotions.

"This is dangerous," I murmured to Auden.

A lonely, average orphan girl like me could get lost in those feelings so, so easily, and I refused to fall for the wrong guy or someone who would only hurt me. I deserved better, and honestly, I'd lost so much that I wasn't sure I could handle more pain.

He shushed me again, so I shut up.

After a moment, he murmured slowly, "The air smells like rain, with a hint of spices you don't recognize, but they set you at ease. To your left, a sapphire-blue ocean moves lazily, at its leisure. To your right, grassy hills of a sparkling emerald roll at different heights and angles. Out in front of you lies a city, one embedded in the hills themselves as doors of varying shapes and colors lay set into the grass, as if they grew there naturally."

I didn't know if the mental image was right, but it was building.

"Above your head, the sky's a soft lavender. The clouds sparkle like the scales on your tail gleam within the blue waters. The breeze ruffles your hair, carrying soft diamond ribbons around your face, while your t-shirt tickles your arms and thighs."

Okay, the mental image was getting stronger. Much stronger.

It was probably just a fantasy, but—

"Hold that," he instructed me softly, his fingers leaving mine. "You're going to take us there."

A sharp pain cut into my shoulder opposite the infected one, much smaller and shallower than the last time I'd been cut. A soft cry escaped me, and a rough hand moved gently up my arm, comforting me.

"Taste the sweetness in the air." Auden's voice remained gentle, a soft stroke of words against my neck as he lifted my fingers to the small cut he'd made in my skin. Dampness coated them, and he held them back out. "See the way the breeze tugs at the red and orange feathers of those golden-winged wind fae, and speak the words, *reducha worless*."

I whispered the words, trying to hold on to that mental image as I spoke them.

As if that was the final piece in the puzzle that fell into place, I felt magic whoosh out of me, a soft tug through the cut on my shoulder.

"Good." Auden's approval was felt more than heard. "Open your eyes."

My gaze landed on a portal. It was smaller than the one Ien had created earlier, but also tugged less on my magic, and it looked prettier too.

Through the center of it, I saw the real version of the place Auden had described to me. It was identical to the image my mind had conjured, and my lips parted a bit.

How had I known what it would look like?

"Avalon belongs to you now, November. It's yours to keep, hold, and protect."

It sounded like I was more married to Avalon than to Auden.

He let go of me and stepped up to my side, his hand catching mine. "I'm not getting left on your awful planet. Let's go."

And just like that, the romance died.

Yeah, I really needed to remember that the feeling he'd given me wasn't from him—it was from our magic.

After one last glance over my shoulder at the islands I'd flooded, I stepped with him through the portal.

Welcome to Avalon, I guess.

CHAPTER 27

EVERYTHING around us was exactly as he'd described.

Emerald grass.

Sapphire water.

Lavender skies.

A smell that made me feel like I was home, with just a hint of spices I didn't recognize.

Rolling hills.

A calm ocean.

Sparkling clouds.

I hadn't been many places or seen many things, but I could definitely say it was the most beautiful place I'd ever laid my eyes on.

Auden inhaled deeply, his shoulders relaxing in a way I'd never seen them relax before.

A massive man with shining, sunflower-yellow hair and dark skin dove through the sky, toward us. Shimmering golden feathered wings stretched out around him, larger and more delicate-looking than the jewel-like reptilian dragon wings of the sky fae.

I started to step backward... until Auden laughed.

The noise startled me, and I jerked away from him.

Since when did Auden know how to laugh?

He released my hand, striding up to the yellow-haired fae and throwing his arms around the guy for a massive, back-slapping man-hug.

Apparently guys hugged like that even in Avalon.

"Rollen," Auden said warmly.

"King Auden," the sunflower-haired man, Rollen, stepped away from my blond king wearing a massive grin, and feigned a bow that had Auden snorting. "I thought the humans would've found a way to end your miserable life by now."

The words didn't sound like a joke, but Auden gave a rumbly chuckle that did weird things to the parts of me that were positive that the king was all glares, anger, and hatred.

"They tried."

Rollen's gaze landed on me, and his eyebrows shot upward. "What the wist?"

That word again.

I really, really needed a definition for it.

"Is that a wisting *faery*?"

So many wists. So little explanation.

Arrgh.

"Hi." I gave Rollen an awkward wave. "I'm Noa."

The man knelt in front of me.

Like, literally, *knelt*.

My eyebrows shot upward.

I began, "You really don't need to—"

"She's mine." Auden's voice was a bit gravelly as he grabbed his friend by the shirt and dragged him to his feet. "King Rollen, meet November. My *kompel*."

Rollen's eyebrows shot even higher than mine. "*Kompellos?*"

"The wister, Ien, is to blame," Auden muttered, turning away from me and striding off toward the hill-city.

Rollen remained where he was, and I glanced between him and Auden, not sure who I should follow or where I should go. Both men were kings, but Auden was the one who I was still bonded to. He had to be in pain, now that we were apart... but he was the one who'd walked away from me.

"Do you search for lovers?" Rollen asked, tilting his head to the side.

"No." All positive feelings I'd had toward the guy suddenly up and vanished. "And if you proposition me, I'll kick you in the balls."

I wouldn't, but he didn't know that.

Taking off toward Auden at a jog, I breathed in Avalon's air. My lungs expanded, feeling like they were clearing and filling in a way they never had before. Whatever tension had existed in my shoulders, eased.

Auden was right; Avalon was home.

I stopped in my tracks, suddenly remembering all of the things I'd left in the beach house.

Photos.

Memories.

Everything that connected me to my grandpa.

My chest started to hurt again, but a different ache than the one Auden's death had caused.

This one wasn't magical pain—it was actual, real grief and loss.

And it stole my breath far worse than the stabbing in my chest had.

Tears dripped down my cheeks.

Dammit—I hadn't wanted to cry. I was usually good at grieving in silence, at keeping my eyes dry and suffering when no one was watching. People had accused me of being unfeeling many, many times before.

But when it came to my grandpa, and all of the things that reminded me of him, and the sharp pain of losing him... I was a teary-eyed mess.

Bending over, I planted my hands on my knees as if I was playing basketball or something, and sucked in Avalon's refreshing air in an attempt to free myself of tears and sadness and chest-ache that I had never completely banished since I buried my grandpa.

"Noa?" Rollen bent over, his face appearing in my line of sight. Concern wrinkled his otherwise-perfect skin. "Whoa. Are you crying?"

"No. I'm fine." My eyes squeezed shut.

Damn the fae and their intruding and their awe at seeing boobs.

"I wasn't propositioning you—I'm sorry that I offended you. It was a test; I didn't expect you to cry. Auden is my brother, and I was just looking out for him." His voice raised. "Auden! Your queen is crying!"

"Shut up," I hissed, through a clenched jaw.

The last thing I wanted was my angry *husband* showing up and getting mad at me for having feelings again.

Straightening, I swiped at the lingering water on my face as I forced myself to get it together. Now was not the time to cry.

Auden had said that faeries could create portals back and forth between worlds; I would just portal back to Avalon Island and see what I could save from the wreckage I'd caused.

Squeezing my eyes shut, I pictured the beach house on Avalon Island, exactly the way I'd remembered it. No one had said that faeries could create portals going to Earth, but how else would they have gotten there to retrieve human men, like Auden's legend said they had?

"What are you doing?" Auden's voice was hard as it interrupted me.

"Going back for my things," I said fiercely, daring him to argue. "The things in that beach house are irreplaceable to me. This is your home, not mine."

Auden's eyes darkened, and Rollen cleared his throat.

We both looked at him.

"She was crying," Rollen said, *so* helpfully.

"About what?" Auden asked him.

"I'm right *wisting* here," I shot back, even throwing that stupid word at them like I knew what it meant.

"You won't admit to me what you're crying about," he growled at me.

What, because of that one time I hadn't?

"Because I'd prefer not to have it thrown in my face the next time you're pissed at me for existing."

"Are all faeries this angry?" Rollen asked.

Auden and I both yelled, "NO!" at the same time.

And then glared at each other.

Rollen cleared his throat. "Well, I'll just accompany the lovely Noa back to Earth for a moment, and all of this will be taken care of."

"No." Auden's voice was sharp. "She has my magic. All of it. And she's been infected by all of the sea, earth, and sky fae. She needs rest, and we need to send out a hunting party."

There was a long, drawn-out pause.

"Apparently we have a lot to discuss." Rollen glanced at me. "Would you be willing to allow a few of my men to retrieve your things? You'd have to make a portal for them to get back, but you could create it here and simply hold it open for a few minutes while they find everything."

I waited for Auden to shoot that idea down too, but his expression remained stony.

"Yeah, I guess. That's fine." I jerked my head in a nod.

He nodded. "I'll find a few volunteers and meet you at your house."

My house?

He strode away, off to find some guys to go on the trip for me. It probably would've been faster to go myself, but Auden was apparently opposed to that.

"My house?" I asked Auden.

His scowl reminded me way too much of the way things had been on Earth, before he'd started telling me necessary things.

Turning, he walked toward the sea.

Swearing under my breath about him and his obnoxiously-stubborn silence, I followed him.

WE DIDN'T WALK FAR, stopping at the hill nearest to the ocean. A simple white door sat embedded in the hill, and Auden threw it open like it belonged to him.

The thought reminded me of that ridiculous fae rule—everything that was Auden's had become mine when we were married.

So the hill probably did belong to him.

We stepped down five stairs, into a light, airy space. All it held was a massive bed, a rack of shirts and pants, and a small room that held a normal-looking toilet and a small sink. No shoes, no closet, no kitchen...

It was odd.

But not uncomfortable; just a different style of home than I was used to.

"Welcome home," Auden drawled, flinging his hands out at his sides.

"Stop." My voice was frustrated, edging on anger. "Why are you being like this again? We've already decided to be friends, and it feels like we just took a major step back and I don't know why."

He'd gotten angry after his friend knelt in front of me—but why? There wasn't a chance it was jealousy, since we weren't in love or anything. So what about the conversation had pissed him off so badly?

"You still refuse to tell me why you were crying," he growled at me.

That clearly wasn't the main reason he'd gotten pissy, but you know what? I was willing to share, on the off chance that it could get us back to where we had been before portaling into Avalon.

"My grandpa was the only family I had for the last decade, and he's only been gone for a year and a half now. Sometimes, I miss him so badly that I just *cry*, okay? Grief is weird; it affects all of us differently. And I hate the way it affects me this time around, but that's just what happens."

His anger seemed to drain away. "That's why you want your things from Earth?"

"Yes. My photobooks are there, along with a few knives he gave me, and a few other trinkets of his. If I'm stuck here for the rest of my life, I want those memories here with me."

Auden's head bobbed.

I guess all he'd wanted was the truth.

He promised, "We'll get them back."

Surprisingly enough, I believed him.

"How are we going to find the other fae and get Hannah and Elyn back?" I pressed. "What are we going to do now?"

"We'll get your things before the water washes them away, and then we'll talk with Rollen, Kilo, and Froet while we come up with a plan."

"What plan could the wind fae help with?" I gestured to the world outside the hill, since the door still sat open. "You said the earth, sky, and sea fae are the strongest and have the biggest numbers." He had also said that any time the wind fae went to war, they won. But I didn't think pointing that out would get me more answers.

"The wind fae have their secrets." Auden glanced out the door as the other king approached. "And for now, our only plan will revolve around hunting and slaughtering fae to cure your infection."

My nose wrinkled at the phrasing. "Hannah and Elyn need to be the priority. They're in the most danger."

"No, they aren't. The kings were speaking the truth when they considered options other than murder for their queens, and Hannah and Elyn are smart enough not to give the magic back without guaranteeing their safety first."

"They might not have a choice, though."

"Torture is off the table for the queens; it will screw with the kings' emotions thanks to the *kompeleno*. They have at least a few weeks before Ien comes up with a workaround or convinces them that a life alone and in pain is worth it. You don't have that long."

"And you're convinced a life alone and in pain *isn't* worth it?" I checked, still wanting validation that he had absolutely zero plans that involved ending my life.

He scowled at me as Rollen and two other fae appeared at the door. "Ready?" the wind king checked.

"Yep." I stepped past Auden, heading up the stairs. As

the men beside the other king gawked at me and my clothing, I glanced down at myself.

Could've been worse.

I was still wearing one of my Tom's Garage shirts over a simple powder blue bikini, but the shirt was long enough to cover my ass at least.

"Hi," I told the men staring at me like I was an alien.

And I guess if it was their first time meeting a woman, I probably did resemble an alien. Especially with all that hair.

"Breathtaking," one of the men said, his tone drenched in shock.

"She's mine," Auden growled at them, catching up to me as I crossed the house.

It was the second time he'd said that, and I didn't know what that was all about because he wasn't possessive of me. He was probably just worried I'd decide to cheat on him with his friends and therefore shame him or something.

"How'd a bastard like you get so lucky?" the other new guy asked, shooting Auden a grin.

"He didn't get lucky. I was the last pick of the three human sacrifices," I shot back.

Yeah, I was pissy. I needed food and a nap, and instead, I was going to hold a portal open for twenty minutes while some other guys went through my things instead of just letting me do it.

But at least I'd be getting my stuff.

"You weren't the last pick," Auden growled.

"Seriously? The other kings picked the other two girls,

leaving you with me. The first thing you did was insult my name. Don't lie to me."

He made a noise of disagreement, but his friends interrupted our argument.

"Noa, this is Kilo and Froet," Rollen introduced me.

"Hi." I gave them an awkward wave.

The subject quickly launched into what I needed them to retrieve. I opened the portal with only a tiny bit of help from Auden—he cut me and told me the words to say again—and soon enough, I had a soggy bag of stuff in my arms.

Auden's friends left soon after that, giving us *time to rest*, and I carried my stuff back into Auden's house.

CHAPTER 28

"So should I unpack my stuff here, or are we moving to the sea fae land?" I asked Auden.

"I don't know," he growled.

He was just as pissy as I was, so we were not at a good place friendship-wise at the moment.

I gave him an exasperated look, dropping my bag on the floor so it didn't soak the bed.

He glared at me. "I was the king for less than an hour before we were thrown out of Avalon, so excuse me for not knowing exactly what's going to happen next."

I didn't want to fight, but I had a lot of shit to say.

Instead of spewing verbal poison, I shut my mouth and dropped to my knees on the floor. Unzipping my bag, I pulled out a few soaked swimsuits—retrieving those had been Auden's idea, and a good one at that—followed by a couple of pocket knives.

Dread hit me when I pulled out the first photo album.

My hands shook, and I tried to talk myself into opening it for a solid minute.

Nope.

I didn't want to see the horrible damage.

Auden kneeled beside me, plucking the album from my hands. The cover opened, and my eyes shut tightly.

I didn't want to look the wreckage in the face.

It was my fault; there was no one to blame but me, except maybe the fae bastards who had given me no other way to protect myself.

A large hand connected with mine, and I tried to hide my surprise.

Was he trying to comfort me?

"Imagine just a little of my power flowing back to me," he murmured. "Not much—just a little."

"No cutting required?"

"No. The magic knows where it belongs."

I willed a gush of the magic that had been transferred into me to move through my arm, back to Auden.

It moved faster and obeyed better than the ocean had.

Auden let out a slow breath, releasing my hand a moment later.

"If you're not going to kill me, you might as well take it all back. I don't know how to use it."

"You still don't trust me not to kill you?" he grumbled.

The air grew a bit more humid, and I glanced over at him as he flipped the pages of the album.

My lips parted as he dried the pictures, removing all traces of water from the plastic film holding the photos.

Some were slightly damaged, but most of them still looked mostly fine.

My throat welled up as he flipped the last page. He handed the album back to me before reaching into the bag and grabbing another album. I had three in total, and all of them were small, but they meant a lot to me.

He quickly dried the other two, then dried everything else inside the bag, and then dried the bag itself.

Standing wordlessly, he walked over to his hanging clothing rack and grabbed a pair of pants and a shirt before stepping into the small bathroom. A man as big as him getting dressed in that tiny bathroom couldn't have been an easy feat, but he didn't complain.

I brushed a hand over my face.

I shouldn't have been a bitch to him.

He was difficult, and I was difficult, and the whole situation was messy and just *difficult*.

Even if that was way too many *difficults* in one sentence.

But I probably owed him an apology.

Since, you know, we were being friends.

I definitely owed him a thank-you, too, since he'd fixed the problem I'd created and all.

Climbing to my feet, I crossed the small room and leaned up against the wall outside the bathroom, waiting for him. He stepped out a second later, and stopped when he saw me waiting.

"Thank you." I gestured over my shoulder. "For helping with that. It means a lot to me. Those things are all I have left of my grandparents, and they..." I swallowed roughly, suddenly emotional.

Dammit, I hated getting emotional.

"They mean a lot to me," I said, stumbling over the words I knew I'd already said. "So, thank you." I paused. He started to say something, but I cut him off before he could, surging forward with that *wisting* apology I owed him. "And I'm sorry, I was being a bitch earlier. I know you were forced into the arranged marriage thing the same way I was, and I shouldn't be angry with you for it. The past is in the past."

"Is it?" he asked, his eyes flashing. They looked a little different now that we were in Avalon; had a little more depth, and sparkled a lot more. "You're still hurt because of it."

I crossed my arms uncomfortably. Was that him rejecting my apology? "It's just stupid sensitivities."

"Ien's plan revolved around killing you as soon as we returned to Avalon. The other kings weren't choosing the woman they found the most attractive; they were choosing the one they were most willing to lose or sacrifice. I wasn't willing to kill any of you, so yes, you were the last pick. The one the other kings least-desired to kill."

I blinked at him.

That was... unexpected.

I should've put that together, I was just too busy being butt-hurt about being the last choice again.

"Wow."

"Not what you expected?" he drawled.

"I thought you were choosing wives."

"How very human of you." He stepped past me, heading up the stairs. "Come on. Your stomach will stop growling after a swim."

My hands lifted to my stomach, and it rumbled as if on cue. "Whoops."

"You used a lot of energy on those portals. You need to swim and sleep, and then we'll figure out the plan." He stopped at the top of the staircase, watching me ascend the steps. "And November?"

"Hmm?" I was officially feeling like crap for assuming the worst of him at every turn.

"Thank you for getting me back home."

The words were simple, but I could tell he meant them.

"So are Rollen, Kilo, and Froet the friends you were talking about?" I checked, as we headed toward the ocean.

"Yes. They're the closest thing I have to a family." He led me down over the grass. He didn't seem to worry about stomping all over it, so I assumed that wasn't a big deal in Avalon.

"Are there a lot of sets of brothers here?" I asked.

"No. Merzo and Kalus are rare; most families were destroyed in the war that ended the faeries, as far as I know."

"And you know a lot," I said.

"I haven't been killed in many years, and dying affects your memory, so yes."

"You just died," I pointed out.

"All of my memories are stored within you and my magic, now."

Well, that was nice, I guess.

"So having faeries return... how does that affect Avalon?"

"That, I don't know." We reached the beach. "Avalon's waters have their own will. You won't be able to control them the way you controlled the oceans on earth. If you're angry, they won't care or react—they're strong, and independent."

"That's a relief."

"It's much easier," he agreed.

The water met my toes as we walked into it, and I stopped abruptly on the beach. A calm, peaceful feeling washed over me. My eyes closed, my head tilting back as that soft, spicy-scent I didn't recognize seemed to grow stronger. "Wow."

"That's the smell of the sea. It'll call to you wherever you go," he murmured.

"It feels so nice."

"It resonates with the magic in your blood, bones, and soul."

"I thought my soul was human," I remarked, wading out into the water with him.

"It became a part of Avalon when you became my *kompel*."

Well, I didn't hate it. That was for sure.

"Take a look at your tail when you're under the water," he told me, before submerging fully in the water and vanishing.

I followed him under, inhaling water. The taste of it was familiar, but new at the same time.

It coated my throat, flowing out through the gills on my abdomen that still felt alien to me. My hunger dwindled, my body feeling stronger as I swam a bit deeper.

When there was more space to move, I flicked my tail up so I could see it, and my mouth dropped open.

No longer did it just glitter and shimmer; now, it looked like it was made out of solid, faceted diamonds.

"Holy crap," I breathed into the water, moving my tail from side-to-side and watching it glitter as the sun that shone through the water hit it at different angles.

Auden appeared in my line of sight, wearing a grin.

My heart legitimately *hurt* at how gorgeous he was when he grinned.

My eyes caught on his tail—glittering even more than mine, as it was longer.

Another breath left me.

It was absolutely incredible.

The way it sparkled, it looked like one massive diamond covering him, cutting down into a fin that somehow also managed to look like an ultra-thin gemstone.

My gaze met his, and I felt my lips lifting in a shocked smile.

He gestured me toward him, and I followed as he headed deeper into the sea.

At first, I just stayed behind him as he darted through the ocean, his tail long and powerful as he led me down deeper.

We cut through caves and wove through a massive coral reef, passing fish of all sizes, shapes, and colors.

Deeper and deeper we went, until he slowed and led me into another cave.

The entrance was smaller, but after a few minutes through a barely-wide-enough tunnel, it opened up into a much larger space.

Shock hit me hard as my gaze slid over the inside of the cave. Soft yellowish-white lights were scattered over the dark walls, shining like stars in all different sizes.

Auden swam to the side of the cave, draping his tailed-body over a rock with a dip in it that looked surprisingly comfortable. When he gestured me over, I pointed to my chest, feigning shock.

His lips tilted up a tiny bit, forming the tiniest of smiles as he dipped his head in a nod.

I swam over, and he scooted to the side to make space for me. I wiggled down, trying to make my tail work with me instead of against me as I settled into place. The rock was smooth, the feel of it silky against my back. There was space between Auden and I, but only a tiny bit. If I moved much, our skin would brush.

If we'd really been married, I would've snuggled into his side and embraced his warmth. I wasn't cold, really, but I definitely wasn't warm—and I'd accidentally brushed my skin against Auden's enough to know that he *was* warm.

We sat there for a long while, staring up at the thousand glittering lights. They moved a bit, twinkling as they did, and a sort of awe nestled in beside the peace that had me relaxing against a rock, beside a man I still didn't really know.

I felt a soft brush against some invisible part of me, and then Auden's words, like a breath in my mind. *"I used to come here to think."*

I tried to speak back, but couldn't figure it out, and frowned.

His lips curved up just a tiny bit. *"Reach your mind out toward mine."*

I had no idea what that meant, but dutifully closed my eyes and tried to mentally reach for him by speaking his name in my mind repeatedly.

A silent chuckle washed over me, and my eyes popped open. *"You don't have to yell."*

I stopped repeating his name.

"There you go."

"How?" I wondered.

"It's called wisting. Only kompells can do it."

I was pretty sure *kompells* meant spouses.

And finally, an answer as to what that word meant.

"Why is it a swear word?"

Another brush of his chuckle washed over me. *"Because it was lost with the faeries. And because wisting was mostly used for sexual activities. This is the simplest form of it—there are stronger ways for kompells to combine their magic and energies that are far more intimate."*

"Oh." I paused, running right over that sex part without mentioning it. *"So we could communicate like this anywhere?"*

"If we wanted to. It'll take some time before we can manage it without the ocean and complete silence."

I nodded.

We both quieted, staring up at the stars.

"Do you miss your piano?" he asked.

The question surprised me. Most people didn't really understand just how important my music was to me, or they thought it was stupid that it meant so much.

"My own piano? Yes and no. I liked it, but mostly, I just liked playing music on it. I'm not really attached to the piano itself—just to the music."

He nodded thoughtfully.

I didn't want to think about the piano left in the earth castle. I'd never retrieved it like I'd planned to, and now it was probably ruined by the flooding I'd caused.

"After we've figured out where we're living and get everything sorted with the infection and the other queens, I'll drag a piano back through a portal for you." His words were simple, but the promise felt solid.

And... it touched me.

"Do that, and maybe we'll really be friends," I teased.

His lips curved up in a smirk.

We didn't speak again, simply staring up at the underwater-version of stars for a long while.

When I eventually yawned, Auden murmured into my mind that it was time to go, and we headed back to the shore.

CHAPTER 29

THERE WAS a covered tray of food waiting beside a card that said, "LUCKY" when we got back to Auden's house. I grinned, and he rolled his eyes with enough of a smirk to tell me he thought it was funny too.

We ate it quickly, and then crashed. He took the floor without a word, and I starfished over the massive mattress. I probably should've offered to share the bed with him, but we definitely weren't at that point in our friendship yet and he didn't ask.

I did throw him a pillow, though.

When I heard him tossing and turning a few minutes after I got in bed, my conscience got the best of me and I scooted to the edge of the mattress, peering over the side. I found Auden smashed up against the side of the wooden frame holding up the mattress, his eyes closed and his expression frustrated.

Feeling a bit sneaky, I pretended to be asleep and dropped

my hand over the edge of the bed. It hit his face and I acted boneless, letting it hang there.

He didn't move for a minute, and then slowly, turned so that my hand rested on his bicep.

A few minutes later, we were both asleep.

"NOA," Auden shook the bed, same as always.

I groaned at him, same as always, too.

"It's time to get up and figure things out." The bed dipped a bit as he sat down near my feet. "And change. You stink."

I mumbled incoherently and ducked my head into the neck of the t-shirt, sniffing at my pits. "I don't stink," I complained at him, sticking my head back out through the neck-hole. His expression was devious. "Which you already knew."

"Mmhmm." He poked my foot, and I barely yanked it away from him fast enough.

"I'm getting up." I swept my hand toward him, shooing him. "How do we wash our clothes here?"

"Dip 'em in the ocean."

Well, that was easy, I guess.

I grabbed an armload of clothes and walked up the stairs. He followed me, trying to take some of them, and I held them away from him.

"You definitely haven't qualified for underwear-carrying yet, buddy," I warned.

"I'm the one who bought them for you," he pointed out.

"Which I'm grateful for. But now that they've been worn, you're fired from them. Those are real-husband privileges, not arranged-husband ones."

"How about friend ones?" he countered.

I snorted. "If you think I let my guy-friends carry my panties around, you're full of it."

"Guy-friends?"

I guess I probably hadn't mentioned them before. "Yeah. I make friends with guys more easily than I do with girls." I shrugged a bit. "All of them left to go live with their families when all of the unnatural disasters started happening, though. So none of them were around when the government sacrificed me."

Auden didn't look entirely sure how to feel about that.

Since I wasn't sure how he should feel about it either, I didn't acknowledge it. They were just my friends, like he was just my friend... what was there to worry about?

CHAPTER 30

I NOTICED QUITE a few winged fae soaring over our heads —probably listening in on our conversation, too. They were all just curious about me, I was sure. Consider the way a group of single women reacted when one decently-attractive man walked into a room with them, the response wasn't surprising. Curiosity was normal, and probably, healthy.

If they'd been too afraid of Auden to fly overhead gawking at me and checking me out, then I would've needed to worry about the man I'd gotten myself married to.

I noticed him eyeing the other fae as he sat on his ass on the beach, legs sprawled out in front of him. His body position made him look relaxed, but I could tell he wasn't.

"Can you still lie?" he asked me.

"I don't know; I haven't tried."

His silence told me to try.

"I'm not worried about the—" the words caught in my throat. I coughed, choked, wheezed, and ended up bent in half, barely maintaining my hold on the bikini bottoms in my hand as I tried to catch my breath.

Auden was on his feet in an instant, coming to my side. He pounded my back, trying to clear my airway for me as I wheezed.

"Crap. You weren't kidding about that," I rasped.

"Nope. Guess you're a full faery, now."

Wow. That was a lot to take in. "Guess so."

I'd been lying when I told Rollen that I was fine the day before, but... well, no. That wasn't a lie. I was emotional, and worried, but I was still *fine*.

He took my bikini bottoms from my hand, plucking a couple more bits of my clothing out of my hands before wading out into the water with him.

"About the lie you told the other fae..." he trailed off. Trying to think of a way to talk about it without triggering whatever fae magic prevented us from lying, I assumed.

"What about it?"

"If you can keep it going without full-on lying, I think you should."

Oh.

He wanted his friends to think we were sleeping together, too?

To prevent more propositions, I was game. "I'll come up with something. You have to make me sound good, if they ask, though. I don't want anyone thinking I'm getting better than I'm giving."

He snorted. "You're the only faery they've seen. That's not what they'll be thinking."

Probably true.

"But you'll still do it," I warned, washing off the last half of my clothes since he'd taken the first half.

Guess I didn't care as much as I thought about him washing my underwear.

"I will." He used his magic to dry off my clothes, then stuck them back in my bag before trying to take the rest of the clothing from me.

I hip-bumped him to block him, and a rasped laugh escaped him as he stumbled after the impact.

Damn, he had a good laugh.

"So where do you think the rest of the fae are?" I asked him, carrying the rest of the clothes back to the bag. He dried them for me on my way, without taking them from my hands.

"Depends who opened the portal."

I didn't have to think hard about that one. "Ien."

"Then I'd say they're probably running rampant in my new kingdom. They'll probably be bleeding one of the other kings, trying to establish one of your friends as a full faery so they can go back to get you from earth."

Rollen strode toward us, but Auden didn't turn away from the conversation, so I pressed him for more details. "But won't they assume you'd bring me back here?"

"Probably. But they don't know how powerful I actually am, and they'll assume that portal they created exhausted you. So they'll think they have at least a little time while you rest."

I frowned. "You're that powerful?"

"Well right now, you're the powerful one," Rollen said flippantly.

Auden grabbed a ball of sand, soaking it and tossing it at the intruder as I shoved my clothes back into their bag. Rollen blasted it back at Auden with a grin, and Auden shot it back at the wind king.

I watched the exchange as a friendly game of catch turned into a full-out mud war. Auden chucked more mud balls into the fight, Rollen blasted them back or turned them into sand, and somehow, both of them ended up coated in mud and grinning.

Rollen slapped Auden on the back... and then threw a mud ball at me.

It hit me square in the left boob.

"Ouch," I complained.

Both men busted up laughing, like freakin' teenagers.

I hated how much I loved it.

"Do breasts have feeling? I thought they were like... squishy lumps of fat," Rollen remarked, gesturing to the air as he pretended to squish it.

I snorted. "You would be terrible in bed."

"I could please any woman," he drawled, still grinning madly. "Now answer the question.

"The boobs themselves aren't normally sensitive, but the nipples are. And that's all I'm saying on the matter. Auden could probably give you some better advice on the topic." I winked.

Voila, there was my anti-lying attempt at telling everyone we were doin' it.

"You're sharing a bed?" Rollen's eyes grew mischievous.

"Are we?" Auden tossed me a smirk.

Clever.

So, so clever.

I could definitely get used to having a partner in crime like that.

I shot him a saucy grin back.

Whether or not he decided to tell his friend the truth about us in private, I knew we had a much bigger audience in the sky. And that was who we were really talking to.

"I'm going to go change. Meeting afterward?" I asked Rollen, wading out into the water a bit to rinse mud off my boob.

"Sure. We're rescuing the other queens, aren't we?" He asked, a gleam in his eyes.

"Yes. They're married, though." He'd better have seen the warning in mine.

"I pity the woman married to Kalus or Merzo," Rollen remarked.

Yeah, I kind of did too.

"Come on, kompel," I tossed the fae word for husband or partner at Auden, along with a smirk.

"I don't want to miss you getting dressed," he drawled, catching up to me and plucking the duffel bag off my shoulder. I wasn't even sure who the duffel belonged to, but it was mine, now.

And I didn't know where his thoughts went to mentally get himself around the lying thing with that sentence, but I wasn't questioning it.

"Exactly."

We'd only just made it a few steps off the beach when someone overhead yelled, "Mermen incoming from the north!"

Someone else shouted, "Centaurs and dragons too!"

Auden halted, spinning toward Rollen. His hand wrapped around my bicep, holding me beside him.

"I guess they've finally realized how powerful you are," Rollen remarked, flashing Auden a beastly grin. "We'll wipe that infection out of your queen in no time. Kilo has the armies; take care of your *kompel*."

Auden's head jerked in a nod.

He grabbed me around the waist in one fluid motion, tossing me over his shoulder before he sprinted toward his hill-house.

The door flew open, and he made it down all five stairs in two steps.

"Stay here," he warned, tossing me to the bed. I bounced up in the air twice, but landed in an angry hair-tangle on the mattress.

"You can't fight without me," I shot back, rolling off the bed and hurtling toward him before he could leave. I tripped over my own freakin' feet before I reached him, and he caught me by the arms. "The bond—you can't go far."

He jerked his head in a nod, staring at me with those diamond eyes that had once creeped me out. Now, I found them beautiful. "Give me half of my magic back."

There was a long pause.

Shouting sounded outside, along with the flapping of wings.

"Save half to cushion you from the infection, but give the rest to me," he repeated.

I don't know why, but I hesitated. Since I'd taken the second half of his magic, he'd been... different. Nicer.

He lifted my hands to the sides of his face, holding them to his skin. I was right before; he was really warm. "Come on, November. Trust me."

Did I trust him?

At least, a little?

"Alright." I closed my eyes, swallowed hard, and pushed his magic toward him. It flowed out of me in a rush, eager to get back to its owner. I tried to keep a hold on some of it, but the push I'd given was too much, and all of it drained out of me.

When I opened my eyes, there was something bigger and scarier and more threatening about him. I could feel the magic pulsing inside him... and the empty hollowness straining within me.

"I'll be back after I take care of that infection," he growled, pulling my hands off his face and stepping backward. "And then, we'll go get the queens."

He was gone, the door shutting behind him so fast I barely had time to blink.

AFTERTHOUGHTS

I fought a lot of self-doubt while writing this book. A lot of
fear that it wouldn't sell. A lot of tension, worrying that
people would hate it. It's different, and honestly a bit weird,
and not what I usually do.

But ultimately, I wanted to write it.

And I'm glad I did, even if it tanks and no one reads it and
everyone hates it.

Because I found myself in November Murphy. Bits of myself.
The sad bits. The sarcastic bits. The bits where you just keep
trying, and pushing, even when it feels like life's out to get
you. I find pieces of myself in all of my characters, but never
as many as I've found in Noa.

I don't know if most of my characters would be my friends in
real life... but I can say without a shadow of doubt that if she
were real, we would be besties.

I've never successfully written an enemies-to-lovers book. I've
tried before, but I just like good guys and hate assholes too

much to write them in as realistic love-interests, and realistic relationships are pretty much my main goal in everything I write. But because of their situation, Noa and Auden needed to be enemies-to-lovers... and I fell in love with the way they interacted.

Although, I do still think the enemies-to-lovers thing should be changed to enemies-to-friends-to-lovers because as I said, I much prefer nice guys.

Anyway, I'm ranting now.

I guess all I really want to say is that these characters spoke to some parts of my soul that I've never before touched before. And seeing as that's my favorite part of being an author—the learning, the growing, the changing—that makes this one of the most challenging, albeit most rewarding, books I've ever written.

And I hope Noa's sarcastic optimism and Auden's angry compassion touched you as much as they touched me.

All the love,

Lola Glass

Please Review

Here it is. The awkward page at the end of the book where the author begs you to leave a review.

Believe me, I hate it more than you do.

But, this is me swallowing my pride and asking.

Whether you loved or hated this story, you made it this far, so please review! Your reviews play a MASSIVE role in determining whether others read my books, and ultimately, writing is a job for me—even if it's the best job ever—so I write what people are reading.

Regardless of whether you do or not, thank you so much for reading <3

-Lola

ALSO BY LOLA GLASS

Sacrificed to the Fae King Trilogy

Shifter Queen Trilogy

Rejected Mate Refuge Trilogy & Standalones

Mate Hunt: Thrown to the Wolves (Kindle Vella)

Shifter City Trilogy (Wolfsbane Spinoff)

Wolfsbane Trilogy & Novellas

Supernatural Underworld Duology

SAY HI!

Check out my reader group, Lola's Book Lovers
for giveaways, book recommendations, and more!

Or find me on:
ETSY
INSTAGRAM
PINTEREST
GOODREADS

ABOUT THE AUTHOR

Teller of stories. Wrangler of children. Buyer of Chinese food. Creator of art. Lover of life.

If that's too vague for you, Lola is a twenty-something with a *slight* werewolf obsession and a passion for love—real love. Not the flowers-and-chocolates kind of love, but the kind where two people build a relationship strong enough to last. That's the kind of relationship she loves to read about, and the kind she tries to portray in her books.

Even if they're about shifters :)

Made in the USA
Las Vegas, NV
28 March 2022

46417989R10167